The Thousand Dollar Man

J.T. Brannan

GREY ARROW PUBLISHING

First published as an eBook 2015

This paperback edition published in 2016 by Grey Arrow
Publishing

Copyright © 2015 J.T. Brannan

ISBN: 978-1533363572

For Justyna, Jakub and Mia;
and my parents, for their help and support

"The soldiers who didn't come back
were the heroes. It's a roll of the dice.
If a bullet has your name on it,
you're a hero. If you hear a bullet go by,
you're a survivor"
- Bob Feller

"Sometimes when I help people,
other people die"
- Colt Ryder

Prologue

Nuevo Laredo was hell on earth.

It had been years since I'd been out of the States, and this little Mexican border town was doing nothing to reignite my love of foreign travel; I'd had nothing but trouble since arriving here the day before.

To be fair, though, I *had* come looking for it.

And I was in real trouble now – blindfolded and bound, I had no real idea where I was, even if I was still *in* Nuevo Laredo. All I knew was that I was in a building with corrugated metal walls and a smell that took me straight back to my last real job, working as a meatpacker in the largest slaughterhouse in the Midwest. Thousands – *tens* of thousands – of carcasses were processed every day in that terrible place, and the smells that came from the rotten meat that accumulated there had been enough to make a man sick. It had reminded me of Iraq. And now, thinking about it, Nuevo Laredo kind of reminded me of Baghdad; and trust me when I say that *wasn't* a good thing.

As my nostrils reacted to the stench of the place, I wondered if I was in a slaughterhouse once more and silently cursed; after punching out my boss, I'd promised to never set foot in such a place again. But what could I do? My hands were tied – literally.

If it *was* a slaughterhouse, it was clear that the owners didn't believe in the benefits of refrigeration – the place was like a sauna, the heat melting my bones and making it hard to breathe. No wonder the meat was rancid.

The blow came suddenly, out of nowhere, and knocked my head back hard. My skull collided with the metal wall behind me; it felt like it maybe loosened a few teeth as well.

I shook my head to get some of my senses back, my body instinctively curling up in a vain effort to protect myself. I'd had worse over the years though. Much worse.

Besides, if they were going to kill me, I wouldn't be wearing a blindfold. They wouldn't care if I saw them.

As long as I was wearing the blindfold, I told myself, I'd be okay.

The situation was far from pleasant though, the beating starting now in earnest, fists and feet flying in from everywhere. At least if you can see the punches and kicks coming – even if your hands and legs are tied, as mine were – you can tense the right bit of your body in time, take some of the shock out of the blow. With your eyes covered, it makes things a whole lot worse. The punches and kicks come from all angles, hitting all over your body, and the only chance you have is to tense up everything, all the time it's happening. But that's almost impossible, so you tend to relax without meaning to – and then they hit you again.

It wasn't all bad though – one of the punches had elicited a grunt of pain from one of my tormentors. He tried to cover it up, not wanting to show weakness, but I caught it loud and clear. I might have been blindfolded, but my ears were working just fine.

I knew the guy must have cut his knuckles on my teeth. More fool him for not wearing gloves; I always do when I'm on the other end of this routine. The fist isn't exactly the best weapon in the world – the bones are tiny and easy to break, and the skin is too thinly spread over those bones to make it anything other than a poor choice as an impact tool. But it seems like a natural thing to do, and people are slaves to their instincts.

"Tell us," said one of the men, not the one who'd just hurt himself; and I amused myself imagining the other guy in the corner, nursing his bleeding knuckles and trying not to cry. "Tell us who sent you, and we can stop all this," the voice said again, his English heavily accented with the singsong Mexican lilt that betrayed his local background.

I wondered briefly if he was being serious. If I told them, would they stop? It was possible; after all, I was a nobody, a hired hand. They weren't interested in me, only in who was behind me.

At the end of the day though, their promises didn't matter; there was no way in hell I'd talk, no matter what they said. It's not that I'm immune to pain and suffering – although I've experienced so much over the years that I can probably handle it better than most – it was just that this interrogation was too crude to break me. It was only a bit of roughing up, maybe more of a warning than anything else. And I still had the blindfold on.

I didn't answer, just spat out a mouthful of blood; I wasn't sure if a crown came out with it as well.

"Tough guy," the man's voice said, very close to me now, so close that I could smell the pepper and nicotine stench of his breath. "Tough guy, you're gonna tell us everything, sooner or later."

He was wrong; dead wrong. I wasn't going to tell him anything, and they weren't going to do anything too bad to me in return.

Then I felt the man's hand go to my face, grip the blindfold and rip it off.

I was momentarily blinded again, only this time by the light as it assaulted my rested retinas, its intensity magnified by the hours of darkness that had preceded it.

But the damage to my eyes wasn't what worried me, as I took in the blurry shadows of the men stood around me.

No, the damage to my eyes might not even matter for much longer.

There were four men stood around me, plus one

other off to the side nursing his damaged hand. They were tough-looking guys, the type who'd seen a lifetime of violence and were completely inured to it.

Some people tell me I have the same look myself.

But it wasn't the sight of the men which scared me; it was the nature of the building itself, its secrets now laid bare.

It turned out that I *was* in a slaughterhouse, just not the meat-packing kind; all around me, through the dusty heat-haze, I could see bloody, broken human bodies, the life beaten and tortured right out of them.

Some of the corpses were incomplete, hands or even entire limbs missing. Some bodies were missing their heads.

And to make matters worse, no effort had been made to clean up the mess; blood lay in congealed pools everywhere through the concrete-floored, metal-walled charnel house, and some of the dead bodies must have been there for some time, insects devouring the flesh. Eggs had been laid in the rotting human meat, larvae born inside the body, maggots emerging to consume what was left.

At least the source of the rancid stench was no longer a mystery.

One of the men walked away then, to a nearby table littered with tools of the trade, all far more effective than the fist.

My stomach turned as he strolled back towards me, a small chainsaw now in his hands. The others started shouting at me in Spanish, spitting obscenities in my face, encouraging the other man to get started.

The man nodded at them and grinned through a mouthful of gold and empty spaces, one hand pulling the cord, the other steadying the chainsaw as it roared to life.

So this was it – captured and imprisoned in a drug cartel's secret little torture palace, about to be carved up and left for the critters.

I shook my head as I thought again of the young girl I'd been sent south of the border to find, saddened and angry that it was all over, her parents never to find the closure they so badly needed.

My blindfold was off.

I was going to die.

PART ONE

CHAPTER ONE

TWO DAYS EARLIER

"So you're the Thousand Dollar Man," the woman said, her eyes playing over me, taking in every detail like a vulture. Only this vulture was about five two and a little over a hundred pounds, with curves in all the right places.

I was in Laredo, Texas – the seat of Webb County, a city of nearly a quarter of a million people just a stone's throw away from Mexico, over the polluted waters of the Rio Bravo which separated them.

I'd made the journey with just my backpack and my dog, Kane; the same way I'd moved around the country for years. I'd discovered Kane early on in my curious second career, during the time I'd taken down a ring of dog-fighting organizers and breeders. They'd been arranging fights to the death for years in the steel towns surrounding Detroit, and – after I'd broken them – one of the puppies had latched onto me. He looked like a German Shepherd, only bigger. I knew there had been a fair mix in his ancestry, and he definitely had some Mastiff blood in him. His back end was higher than a normal Shepherd's, more able to work. And as he grew over the years, he added plenty of muscle to his frame.

He hadn't wanted to leave me alone, and I'd taken him with me; and since then, I'd never regretted the decision for an instant. I was a loner, but it was nice to have company. He was also immensely trainable, and reminded me of the dogs I'd worked with in Iraq and Afghanistan; amazing animals who sniffed out IEDs and drug caches. In fact, military working dogs had been used as sentries, scouts, messengers and searchers; and as far back as Roman times, as dogs of war, trained to attack the enemy.

As he grew into adolescence and adulthood, Kane had performed all these tasks over the years, and was as much a part of me as my arm or leg; I didn't know what I would do without him, and didn't look forward to finding out.

We'd walked the length and breadth of North America since our first meeting, and Kane was my constant companion; my partner, through thick and thin.

We'd only travelled so far south this time – a long way from our normal stomping grounds – to attend a funeral.

Even though I'd been invalided out of the military years before, I still kept my ear to the grapevine, still kept tabs on my old war buddies. Like Jeb Wilkins, a fellow Ranger I'd served with in both Iraq and Afghanistan as members of the Regimental Recon Detachment. He got it before I did, stepped on an IED just outside Mosul back in 2003. Took both his legs clean off, plenty of pelvis too. I'd been with him at the time, had tried desperately to hold bits of him together until the real medics could get there and do their thing.

Between us we must have done something right – Jeb survived and returned stateside soon after, although he'd been reduced to a life of wheelchairs and pissing through tubes ever since.

When he was further north – and when my life had been somewhat closer to "normal" – I used to visit him as much as I could; but since his move to Laredo, I'd not managed to see him at all, never seen the low-rent hostel in the city's poverty-stricken downtown area where he'd spent his final years alone and – it was now all-too apparent – suicidally depressed. He'd been bitter and resentful since the "accident" and I could well understand where he was coming from; I had some of the same issues myself.

But I got there in the end – too late to help perhaps, but with time enough to pay my last respects, joined for the small service by the few people who still knew or cared about him; a few guys from the hostel, and a couple of other buddies from the 75th Ranger Regiment. It was good to see them, even given the circumstances; they were some of the only people left who still knew me as Colt Ryder.

To everyone else – including this stunning Latina woman sitting in front of me – I was the Thousand Dollar Man; not a real person at all, but a mythical character, an urban legend. Many people didn't think I existed at all, despite the exposé a few years back in the *Washington Post* – a piece that was surprisingly accurate, and did a lot to increase my levels of business.

And speaking of business, that's what I was there for, sitting in the beat-up living room of a girl called Gabriela Torres. A living room like dozens I'd seen before, a neighborhood like hundreds; and yet another story of heart-ache and desperation.

I'd seen the sign in the window of a local mom-and-pop grocery store as I'd been strolling the streets of Laredo that morning. I'd been walking off the hangover from the previous night's drinking session with my old Ranger buddies; I'd regretted the pounding in my head that resulted, but it had been the best way to see Jeb off, and we were all sure he'd have had it no other way.

The sign had been simple and direct, as they so often were; there was nothing subtle about it in the slightest. I couldn't blame people though; subtle could often be missed, and they wanted so badly to be heard. I was the last resort, the person others relied upon when they'd tried everything else.

THOUSAND DOLLAR MAN! the sign had screamed at me in red magic marker, *I need your help!*

It had then given a phone number, and I wondered

how many fake calls the person behind the sign had received; kids playing games, curious neighbors, even the police. Probably the number was for a pre-paid cellphone, bought for cash; my clients didn't normally want to advertise who they were by listing their real phone numbers.

Over the years, my clients had told me about all sorts of people who had contacted them, pretending to be me; but what could I do? I didn't invent the system, but had had it thrust upon me both by the public, and by that article in the *Washington Post*.

I'd been wandering across the States for months, helping out whenever I found people who needed helping, when I'd first seen a sign for my services, posted in the window of a truck-stop diner. When I'd spoken to the man who'd placed it, he said he'd heard rumors about me and had decided to take his chances; if I came across it and responded, then fate had decided to be kind to him.

The story must have spread quickly, for a few days later, in a town hundreds of miles away, the same thing happened; another window, another advert for the "Thousand Dollar Man". And then people started taking out ads in the local papers, and I found myself checking the classifieds in every small town I rolled into. And more often than not, there was something for me.

The national press had finally gotten wind of me, and the *Post* article had subsequently described the various ways of contacting me; and now there always something for me, no matter where I ended up.

But that was alright by me; I have a habit of getting bored easily, and in this game, every day threw something different my way.

Some of the people leaving me messages were cranks and crazies, but I soon dealt with them; more dangerous were people setting me up for revenge attacks stemming from the results of earlier jobs. As such, I was very wary of who I met, when, and where. And it wasn't just gangland thugs or angry husbands either; the police were always on my tail for one thing or another too, and were constantly trying to entrap me. But they still weren't able to pin anything on me, despite years of effort.

I'd called the number from a pay phone just minutes after I'd spotted it. I don't carry a cell phone, as it's just one more way for someone to track me, and I try not to use the internet for the same reason. Somebody asked me once why I don't set up an online message board instead of getting people to leave notes in the classifieds, or posters on barroom walls. But I don't like to be "connected" to any more people than I have to be, even if I knew how. I'm kind of old fashioned, I guess. If people want to contact me, they can. They know what to do.

A woman – from her voice, in her late twenties, maybe early thirties – had picked up, and I'd arranged to meet her at a local café. Gabriela Torres was her name, but I took no more details over the phone. Before the meeting I consulted local records and found her home address, then went into surveillance and observation mode.

I'd had no intention of meeting her at the café; it was just a ruse to flush out anyone who wanted to do me harm. I watched her from a distance, Kane at my side; I noted only her beauty at first, then her look of nervous harassment. But nobody else met her there, and there didn't seem to be anybody else watching her either.

I watched until she got bored waiting, then followed her as she paced back to her car – a bust-up nineties Toyota Corolla – and then as she cranked the old beast up and scooted off, presumably back to work. I'd seen the badge on her blouse, glad that it confirmed both her name – Gabriela Torres, she'd not been lying – and where she worked, which was somewhere called the Falcon International Bank.

Satisfied it wasn't a set-up, I'd set off to find where she lived, Kane bouncing along happily by my heels. He'd enjoyed a beer or two last night as well – one of the guys hadn't been able to resist filling his dog bowl with chilled Budweiser – but he seemed none the worse for it now. I put it down to his age – Kane was in the prime of his life, while I was moving steadily past mine.

The girl's apartment was in a four-level building on Salinas Avenue, her unit placed right above a cut-price sports store whose customers didn't appear to do much sport. Must be a fashion thing, I decided; this area was baggy pants and basketball shirts all the way.

Like most of the city, Salinas Avenue was predominantly Latino and my features could well be noted as being out of place; my everyday dress of work pants, army boots and t-shirt didn't exactly mix in with the faux-sportswear that seemed to be the norm here either. But at least I didn't have my fifty-pound backpack – basically my home, all wrapped up in one easy-to-carry package – on me, having left it in a locker at the train station. It might have made me stand out even more if I'd been hefting that thing about the neighborhood.

There were balconies looking out onto Salinas, but the back was a lot more private and – leaving Kane on lookout duties – I managed to gain access to Gabriela Torres' apartment with practiced ease.

I didn't carry a gun, but I wasn't going in unarmed; I had a folding knife in my right pants pocket, and a lightweight expandable metal baton in my left. It might not save me if there was a gang waiting for me, but I'd managed to do more with less in the past.

But as it happened, the place was safe; just a woman's apartment, with no hint that there was anything else going on except someone who wanted my help.

Happy, I left Gabriela Torres' home the way I'd found it and left to wait for her return.

CHAPTER TWO

She arrived home from work a couple of hours later – again, I was pleased to see, with nobody following her – and I went up to her apartment once more, this time from the front.

After a brief moment of anger stemming from me missing our earlier meeting, she agreed to let me in, and I soon found myself sitting on an old sofa in her living room sipping a cup of strong coffee, marveling at how she was even better looking up close.

So you're the Thousand Dollar Man, she'd said just moments before, and I realized that I'd not yet answered, mesmerized instead by her dark, sultry beauty; I checked myself and quickly snapped out of it. Business was business after all, and it paid to pay attention.

"That's what people call me," I said.

"What's your real name?" she asked, her voice low and smooth; I felt it touch me almost as if she was running a hand up my leg.

"I barely remember," I said. "But I'm here to listen to your story. You need me, so what do you want me to do?"

She looked a little hurt, as if aggrieved that I'd managed to survive her seductive charms, but she recovered quickly. "A thousand dollars?" she asked.

I nodded. "Yes."

"Why a thousand?"

"It has a special meaning for me." It was true, but there was no reason to explain it all to her.

"I thought you were a good guy," she breathed, edging closer. "Why charge at all?"

"If I did it for free, the jobs would never stop," I said. "If it was free, everyone would want me to do everything. The thousand dollars is to sort out the people who are serious."

"A thousand dollars isn't much to a millionaire."

"I don't do a lot of work for millionaires."

She smiled at me, and I felt my heart skip a beat. How old was I? *Get a grip*, I told myself.

"Is it true you won the Medal of Honor?" she asked.

It *was* true, and I wondered how she knew; it wasn't in the newspaper article. Probably someone, somewhere, had just made it up, and it had spread like any rumor. This one just happened to be true.

I decided to ignore the question altogether; I didn't

like talking about dead friends.

"So what's the job?" I asked.

"Well," she purred, running a fingertip down the arm of her chair, "it's like this. I'm into ladies, okay? And my girlfriend – my soulmate, the one I'm gonna spend the rest of my life with – she's married, okay? Married to a real loser, but she doesn't see it, she's too scared, and *I'm* scared she'll never tell him, she'll never be free to love me properly. You know?"

I nodded, although in fairness I *didn't* know.

"So what do you want from me?" I said. "Why don't *you* just tell the husband?"

She laughed at that, then shook her head sadly. "Then I'll look like the bad guy, yeah? Chrissie wouldn't *ever* forgive me, and then what would be the point? And her husband's a real piece of work, he'd do a number upside her head, you know? She'd get hurt, and no good would come of it anyway."

My teeth gritted subconsciously at the thought of the girlfriend's husband beating her; some people think of me as a violent man – and perhaps they're right – but men hitting women and children is one thing I can't stand. It offends me beyond reason.

"So what do you want me to do?" I asked. "You want *me* to tell him?"

"Uh-uh," she said with a shake of her head. "I want you to *kill* him."

And there it was; the task I'm often asked to perform. At a thousand dollars, not a bad little investment for some people. The only trouble is, I'm no assassin. I help people, I don't kill them.

"You've got the wrong guy," I said, standing up to leave. "I'm not a hit man."

I started for the living room door and she stood too, put a gentle hand on my arm, encouraging me to stay.

"But I've heard . . . I mean, that article in the paper . . . what people say . . . you *have* killed people."

I turned to her, my six foot frame towering above her petite figure. "Sometimes when I help people," I admitted, "other people die."

That much was true, unfortunately; the sort of men I came across often didn't want their lives to be interfered with, and tried to put me out of business permanently. I tended to respond in the same manner, and – so far – had always come out on top, leaving a body count to reflect it. But that wasn't the point.

"So you *do* kill people," Gabriela said, squeezing my arm.

"Only if they get in my way," I explained. "That's never the job, though."

She nodded. "I guess that helps you sleep at night, huh?"

She'd meant to be sarcastic, but it was true. It *did* help. "Yep," I said. "It helps me sleep like a baby. You've got to have principles, and then you've got to stand by them, or what are you worth?"

She nodded her head finally, in understanding. "Nothing, I guess," she said sadly; and then her fingers were opening, stroking up my forearm, her dark eyes staring up into mine. "But if you don't want to do the job," she purred, "maybe you *can* help me with something else."

Her touch was going higher, her fingers tracing up to my neck, then down to my chest. I kept looking into those doe-like eyes. "What did you have in mind?" I asked her.

"Maybe you could help me get my own back a little," she whispered, as her hand crept even lower. "Maybe make Chrissy jealous a little bit, make her see how it feels. If she has a man, maybe so can I . . . If only for one night."

Her hand reached my belt, and for a moment I considered rejecting her advances; but only for a moment. I'd turned down her offer of a job after all and this, as I saw it, would be the least I could do for her.

As she led me into the bedroom by my belt, I thought that you could maybe call it another one of my principles – helping a damsel in distress.

And you have to stand by your principles, I told myself, or what are you worth?

CHAPTER THREE

I woke up early the next morning, my body stiff and uncomfortable; Gabriela had given me one hell of a workout the night before, and I was suffering for it now. That being said though, I wouldn't have changed it for the world. Whoever Chrissie was, she was a lucky woman, I could definitely vouch for that.

I left Gabriela sleeping in bed, got dressed and slipped out quietly from her apartment. I wasn't one for long goodbyes, and I didn't want to hear any more talk about killing her girlfriend's husband. It wasn't the sort of work I did, and I didn't want to make any more excuses.

I picked up Kane as I went; Gabriela had agreed for him to come up and sleep in the apartment, much to my relief. If he'd had to wait outside, I just knew he'd never forgive me in the morning. It would be the look in his eyes, there'd be no avoiding it. But as it was, he was happy and playful after a good night's rest on the sofa and ready for another day's long walk.

We trotted down the apartment steps to Salinas and took in the view, the early morning streets empty and deserted, only the odd car disturbing the peace. The sun was already rising steadily over the rooftops though, and the heat was building. I knew it wouldn't be long before the denizens of the neighborhood appeared, to make their way to school, to work, or just to wander the streets on the lookout for a new way to make money, legal or illegal; it was just that sort of area, and I knew them well. I'd lived in plenty of them myself.

I'd decided to wander back to the train station today, pick up my backpack and move on out; I'd checked the classifieds already, and there was nothing else keeping me here. Unless I passed another poster on the way to the station, of course; then I might just stick around and see what I could do.

I was going to keep my options open about how I'd leave Laredo; Zapata was fifty miles south, Carrizo Springs was eighty miles north, and Alice was ninety-five miles east, with not a hell of a lot in between. It would be easier to get the train or a bus – but on reflection, I decided that Kane didn't much like public transport. And to be fair, I wasn't a big fan either. After so long alone, I'm not keen on being so close to so many people I don't know. Combat fatigue perhaps; or maybe I'm just plain antisocial. But either way, I'd made my mind up by the time I was halfway along Salinas –

I'd walk to the next town.

It might take me a few days, but what the hell – the weather was beautiful and I'd sleep out under the stars. When I reached Alice I'd get a hotel room and have a long shower, rest up a couple of days – depending on the classifieds, of course – and then move on east to Corpus Christie, check out the beaches on the Gulf of Mexico coastline. Have a vacation maybe.

Kane's body tensed next to me only fractions of a second before I reacted myself, hairs on end; we were being followed.

Kane turned his head and let out a long, low growl and my hand went to the folding knife in my pocket, withdrawing it unseen and hiding it in my palm as I turned.

The man was an aging Hispanic, pants barely containing a large gut, hair thinning on top but making up for it with a thick mustache below. Unlike me, he looked like he belonged here. He was still across the street, well away from us; but Kane and I had both felt it, his eyes on us, his attention crossing the empty street like a laser beam. He tried to hide it as I glanced casually his way, but I knew he'd been watching me. But why?

I carried on down the street, Kane responding to my relaxation and also turning away from the man, close to my heel. I monitored the guy though, watched him watching me, using the reflections of car windshields and storefront windows. He continued to follow us steadily, hiding behind parked cars and lampposts like something out of a Sixties spy movie. I might have laughed if I wasn't so busy wondering what it meant.

The street was widening out in front of me as I headed north, and already the people were starting to come out; traffic was increasing, a few cyclists, early morning dog walkers like me. A big municipal building was up ahead on my right, a small square of park to my left; it was nothing exciting, just a bit of grass and a few trees, but it gave me an idea.

I checked the position of my pursuer one last time – he was waiting to cross an intersection after me, still feigning disinterest – and then I turned abruptly from the sidewalk into the park, disappearing into the shadows.

I rounded a tree – in the same comedy Sixties spy style as the man behind me – and then quickly lifted myself into the branches above, my actions hidden from view. I left Kane sniffing the wide trunk beneath me as I waited for the man to appear, as I knew he inevitably would.

I didn't have to wait long; less than a minute later he was nervously edging round the bole of the tree, face anxious, then horrified as he saw Kane waiting there for him, hackles raised and poised to attack. The man didn't know that my dog would only do so at my command, and the fear reaction caused him to freeze there below me, absolutely immobile.

I used the opportunity to act, dropping down from the branches and forcing the man back against the trunk, my razor-sharp three-inch blade at his throat. Kane left me to it, turning to guard the perimeter.

"Who are you?" I whispered, aware that there were now people out on the streets who might eventually see what was going on. "Why are you following me?"

Panic spread across the man's lined, weather-beaten face, and I wasn't sure if he'd pissed in his pants. This was no Mafia killer sent to track me down and get revenge, that was for sure. Whoever he was, he was way out of his league.

He didn't respond and I repeated the question in Spanish, just in case he hadn't understood.

His own language seemed to relax him, and I saw a little of the fear leave his eyes. There was another slight pause, and then he spoke in his own throaty whisper. "I . . . speak English," he gasped, "and I wish you no harm, you must believe me, please."

I eased the pressure from his throat slightly, and I sensed him relax more. A growl from Kane alerted me to a passerby, and I moved the knife from his throat to a more concealed location at his ribs, moving away slightly so it looked like we might just be chilling out in the park, shooting the shit about last night's game, or how the kids were getting on at school.

"Okay," I said pleasantly, monitoring the young couple who strolled past us arm in arm, glad when they'd passed us by. "Now tell me who you are."

"My name is Emilio Rosales, I live next door to Gabriela Torres," he said rapidly, "and you are the Thousand Dollar Man, no?"

I didn't reply, still wondering what this was all about, and he breathed harder, nervous but wanting to plunge on. "Yes," he continued with half a smile, "I know it is you, it *must* be you. I've waited for so long, and here you are." His eyes opened wider. "I need your help. *Please.* I need your help."

"What sort of help?" I asked, releasing the knife from Emilio's ribs ever so slightly.

"My daughter has gone missing," he said. "I need you to help find her."

I sighed, and pocketed the knife.

Alice and Corpus Christie were just going to have to wait a few days more.

CHAPTER FOUR

I was back in the same four-level apartment block that I'd spent the night in, barely twenty minutes after I'd left.

Emilio hadn't been lying; he did indeed live next door to Gabriela Torres, and had probably had his beauty sleep disturbed by his neighbor's screams the previous night. Maybe by mine, too. But – gentleman that he was – he made no mention of it, and nor did his wife, Camila, who served us black coffee in complete silence. I couldn't be sure if she didn't speak English, or just didn't approve of my being there. Emilio had offered me something stronger, but it was still too early in the day, even for me.

It turned out that they knew Gabriela well, knew all about her problems, knew also that she wanted to hire me. They saw the notice was missing from the grocery store window, noticed me knocking on her apartment door, and put two and two together.

So much for my security, I thought mirthlessly.

It also turned out that Emilio and his wife had long since been after my services too, but were too scared to advertise; and I was about to find out why.

I sipped on the strong coffee and watched as Kane lolled about on the rug in front of us, happy to be living a life of luxury two days in a row; and then Emilio placed his own cup down on the cluttered table in front of us, ready to get down to business.

"You are free for a job?" Emilio asked, eyebrows raised. "You already busy for Gabriela?"

I shook my head. "There was a conflict of interest," I said. "I'm free, depending on what you need."

The look of relief in his eyes was obvious. "Thank you," he said. "Thank you. We were going to put up our own advert, you know, but then Gabriela told us she'd put hers up and, you know . . ."

I waved his explanations away. "There aren't any rules for this sort of thing," I assured him. "You needed me, now you've got me. So tell me what it is you want me to do. You said your daughter is missing."

Emilio nodded, tears starting to well up in his eyes. His wife came in from the kitchen, hands going to his, clasping them to her lap. She remained silent, letting her husband do the talking.

"She was such a good girl," he started, "so happy, so *ambitious*, you know? And around here," he said, gesturing around the apartment, outside to the surrounding neighborhood, "that's pretty special, right? So many kids here are into drugs, guns, gangs, you name it man, they're doing it. End up a mess, one way or another. But not our girl, no way, no way. Little Elena was good all the way through and through."

I listened to the father's story, as I had many times before; the details were different, but the message was the same. Their girl or boy was good, a perfect straight-A student, loved by all; then something happened, they got in with the wrong crowd, went off the rails, did something wrong, got into trouble, or sometimes simply went missing, never to be seen again. And when you start digging, it always turned out that little Trixie or Freddie weren't really the sweet angels their parents painted them to be. Whenever I had a case like that, more often than not I didn't tell the parents exactly what I'd found; most of them were dead, and that was enough heart-ache for any mother or father without destroying the image they had of their child as well. Let them live on in the memory as saints, if that made things easier.

"Anyway," Emilio continued, wiping away a tear, "she . . . I don't know, I guess she might have finally fallen in with a bad crowd, I don't know, something like this, okay? Wait," he said, "let me back it up a little, I . . . This is Laredo, right? Laredo, Texas. Now, across the river we've got a whole other story. *Nuevo* Laredo, Mexico. Just a river and a few little bridges, that's what separates us. A river and a few bridges. And one of those bridges ain't too damn far from here, okay? It's a lot of temptation for a young girl. And we've got some family there, we can get over the border each way, no problems. Now life here ain't exactly paradise, but it ain't too bad, lots of folks here are honest, we work hard, you know? But over the river, it's *wild* – I mean, that's what the kids hear, and that's what they wanna go and find out. Is it like people say? Is it really one long party there?"

"Is that what people say?" I asked, and Emilio nodded his head.

"It's the gangs, see? They want our kids to cross the river, make mules out of them, you know? We can cross back and forth, they want our kids, get them over there without their parents to watch out for them, start them smuggling for them. So they start selling a line of bullshit about free this, free that, party all night long at the clubs, they let teenagers in no problem, you know? Well, who can resist that?"

"You think that's what happened?"

Emilio shrugged. "I don't know. I just don't know. But when she went missing, her friends knew that she'd been planning on going over the bridge, going to a nightclub, seeing what it was all about. I don't know who she went with, and the police don't give a rat's ass on *either* side of the border. But I think she went, yes."

"And the gangs got to her?"

Again he shrugged, and a tear came to his eye once more. "I . . . You know, a part of me hopes she *is* working as a mule," he said in a choked voice.

I knew what he meant; if his daughter had been taken by the gangs in Nuevo Laredo, there was no telling what work they would be forcing her into. From my limited understanding of the situation south of the border, the city had been beset by gang warfare for years, with rival drug factions responsible for massacre upon violent massacre. And it wasn't just drugs, either; gun running, prostitution and human trafficking were all fair game to the cartels.

I knew what Emilio must be thinking; if Elena had been turned into a drug mule, she would have been seen in Texas, as the entire purpose would have been to exploit her family connections and her ease of border crossing. And if she'd not been seen, that meant that the gangs were either using her for something else – and the sex trade would be the most likely destination for her – or she was already dead.

This was again something I often had to deal with – situations where there would be no happy ending. Often all a parent needed was confirmation of their child's death; it would save years of wondering. And in Mexico, the chances were good that she was dead. The cartels didn't hold much stock in the sanctity of human life and thought nothing about murdering innocent people, even children.

I remembered reading about one cartel assassin who'd given up counting after he'd passed his eight-*hundredth* victim. A member of Barrio Azteca, he'd dismembered and beheaded men, women and children just to impress his boss; a boss who'd demanded that his squad kill eight people a *day* just to keep up fear and tension in the area.

For all the public outrage about Islamic State and their beheadings of military personnel and journalists in Iraq and Syria, the terrorist group was a long way behind the Mexican cartels in terms of sheer barbarity. A UN report I'd read estimated that nine thousand civilians had been killed in Iraq in 2014; but the cartels had killed sixteen thousand in 2013 alone, and a further *sixty* thousand in the previous six years. They were responsible for a murder every half an hour for seven years.

And people went missing too, all the time; there was even a name for them, like some sort of national plague – "the lost". Thousands upon thousands of them, and you had to assume that most of them were dead. As an example, a busload of 43 students were kidnapped in 2014 and never seen again, and that was only one single incident. Kidnap and murder were at epidemic levels in Mexico, and I knew that Emilio and Camila would know that too. I admired their courage, their will to see this thing through to the end.

But then again, I considered, there was always the chance that Elena *was* alive somewhere, and maybe she could be found and brought home.

The chance was slim – incredibly slim – but it was there.

In the end, I nodded my head. "Okay," I said, "I'll help you."

Emilio smiled at me, truly grateful, and he gestured

for his wife, who stood and went to a cupboard in the corner of the living room. The gratitude on both their faces pained me, knowing how misplaced it probably was; but I would do my best to put their minds at rest and find out what had become of their girl, at the very least.

Camila returned with an envelope stuffed full of cash, which she handed over to me without a word. I followed suit and received it in silence, putting it in my pants' cargo pocket, the deal sealed. I was their man now, and I would do anything it took to find their daughter, dead or alive.

"Okay," I said as Camila sat back down. "Let's get some more detail on what happened. When did she go missing?"

Emilio looked me straight in the eye as he answered.

"Three years, two months and four days ago," he said.

The news made me stop still, rigid as a statue. *Three years?*

I put down the coffee cup and turned to Elena's mother. "Excuse me," I said, "perhaps I *will* have that stronger drink now."

Three years?

Damn.

I'd thought this one was going to be a bitch anyway, and now it looked like it was going to be one hell of a lot harder.

CHAPTER FIVE

Elena Maria Rosales had been just thirteen when she'd gone missing; she'd be nearing seventeen now, if she was still alive.

Emilio had shown me her room, unchanged since she'd gone – another cliché that was often true.

I had a look around, but I knew there wouldn't be much there. The police had already been through the place with a fine toothed comb and – although it looks good in the movies – a poor dumb freelancer like me rarely finds the hidden clue that solves the mystery. There would be no secret diary here with a list of boyfriends and a play-by-play of Elena's illicit visits to Mexico. If there had been, the police would have found it, no matter how uninterested they were in the case.

And three years later? Not a chance.

And yet I did search, as you never knew –

sometimes a clue might just pop up from nowhere, missed by everyone else.

But not this time – the room was clean. What I *did* pick up was a feel for Elena as a person, from the books on her shelves to the clothes in her drawers, and from the scrawled notes on her desk to the posters on her wall.

She'd been a bright girl, that much was clear – maybe not straight A, but a solid B student at the local high school, supported by report cards her parents showed me. A quiet girl in the seventh grade, her teachers said, just coming out of her shell as she entered the eighth. I wondered, darkly, where that increased sociability had led her.

Photographs showed her to be pretty, but not overly so; just a regular teen, getting used to herself, awkward but at the same time with that confidence of youth pushing on toward adulthood. Perhaps faster than she should have been.

She'd been on a few dates, but she'd had no steady boyfriend when she'd gone missing; at least none that her parents knew of, anyway.

I went back into the living room, not sure that I'd made any progress; what Elena had been like at thirteen was almost certainly not what she'd be like now.

"Who do you think she went over the bridge with?" I asked Emilio.

"I'm not sure," he said, although his eyes told me there was a name there somewhere.

"Come on," I said, "it doesn't matter whether

you're right or wrong, just go with your gut instinct. Who?"

"I don't know why, but I always figured it was a girl called Noemi, a friend of Elena's."

I nodded, making a note of the name. Gut instincts were often right, and for good reason; the human is a survival machine, and the brain is programmed to take in millions of pieces of information and sift through them in instants. We can't process that much information consciously, and so when our subconscious mind has done the job for us, we think it's not logical, that we should ignore it. But sometimes it's the most logical thing of all.

"Last name?" I asked.

"Pineda, I think. I'm not sure." He paused, took the glass of water held out to him by his wife, and drank deeply before continuing. "I guess I didn't know her that well, she'd only been friends with her for a few weeks before . . . you know." He looked up at me. "Hey, maybe that's why I think of her? Because she was new, you know? Elena becomes friendly with her, then . . ."

I *did* know. New people, new experiences. Like crossing the border and hitting the Nuevo Laredo nightclubs at the age of thirteen. Emilio's gut was pretty logical all along.

"Any idea where Noemi lives?" I asked next.

"Well, I think she *did* live over on San Bernardo Avenue, just four blocks east of here. No idea where she'll be now."

"Okay," I said, "I think I have enough to go on for now. I'll be in touch."

"You going to find Noemi?"

"Yes. And from there, we'll just have to wait and see."

Emilio shook my hand and I nodded to Camila in farewell, then I headed out the door.

I wasn't much of a detective, but this girlfriend was as good a starting place as any. I'd found, over the years, that you just needed to start picking away at one corner, and then sometimes something big would start to unravel.

And, going with Emilio's gut instinct, I'd decided that the corner I was going to pick away at was Noemi Pineda.

CHAPTER SIX

The heat of the day was really building now, steam rising off the sidewalks as Kane and I trotted on toward San Bernardo Avenue. But when you've pulled a twelve-hour patrol shift in full body armor in an Iraqi summer, with temperatures rising upwards of a hundred and thirty, everything else feels pretty balmy by comparison. Still, I was glad I'd left my jacket and backpack back at the train station.

I'd called a contact of mine and found that a Pablo Pineda, aged thirty-five, was registered to Iturbide Street, which intersected San Bernardo Avenue. A quick look at Pablo's details confirmed that it was the address I was looking for; the intel showed that he was a widower with two children – a son named Juan, aged nineteen, and a daughter named Noemi, aged sixteen. I presumed Noemi still lived with her father; as a minor, she wouldn't be on the electoral register, but she could still be there. And either way, I hoped Pablo could tell me where she was.

Iturbide Street was similar in style and substance to Salinas, but with the commercial buildings and apartments giving way slightly to regular two-story single-family homes in chain-link fenced lots.

I wasn't really clear on what I was going to do if Pablo was at home; the perfect thing would be if everyone else was out except Noemi, and she couldn't wait to tell me everything about what had happened three years, two months and four days ago.

But I knew life didn't often work out that way, and so prepared myself for the worst.

It seemed that all the homes along Iturbide had dogs protecting them, attacking the fences as we strode past. There was an eclectic mix, but pit bulls seemed to be a definite favorite. Kane had reacted to the first one or two, but now ignored them just the same as I did.

We were getting near now, and already I could hear a ferocious barking from behind the fence of Pablo Pineda's property. A few more feet, and there it was – another pit bull, maybe a brother of half the dogs on Iturbide; only this one was even meaner.

Kane reacted instantly, turning to the threat, but settled down to follow my lead as I remained calm and placid. "It's okay," I told him. "It's okay."

I knew it was important not to let Pineda's dog get even more ramped up by appearing aggressive, or even submissive; that would only make things worse. He was only defending his territory, after all. What I was after was assertive confidence, something Kane could achieve without even trying.

I could see how the pit bull was already reacting to Kane's presence, its fierce raking of the chain-link dampening slightly. But we still had to get in there, and – although I knew not to transmit my fears – I had to admit that it was hard to ignore the images of getting ripped to shreds that were running unbidden through my mind. I took a few seconds, and centered myself by breathing slowly, steadily – in through the nose for a four-count, hold the breath for another four; out through mouth for a four-count, hold for another four, and repeat until calm. After two full cycles, my nerves were steady.

Against a human, I wouldn't have had to even slow down – on the surface, I didn't look afraid at all. But I knew a dog can sense things we can't, can smell fear through the hormones we release when excited or nervous, can tell from our body language exactly what our state of mind is. They're the world's best lie detectors.

Kane looked at me as if wondering what I was waiting for, and then I approached the gate, backing in so as not to make the pit bull feel its territory was being threatened by an aggressor. If I came in strong, the dog might attack. And so I backed in, holding the gate open for Kane.

Kane edged his way over slowly, and I wasn't surprised to see that the pit bull didn't attack; he merely held his ground and growled, barked, then growled again. But he didn't advance, which I knew was a good sign; a truly dangerous dog would have just attacked. This one was just trying to establish some ground rules, see who was who in the pecking order. He stopped growling, but stayed alert as Kane came nearer; and ultimately, he allowed Kane to sniff him, then sniffed Kane back, both dogs trying to figure the other out.

But in the end, the pit bull gave into Kane's aura of assertiveness and submitted; he calmed down and even ignored me as I approached the house.

It never ceased to amaze me, people who had watch dogs. What typically happened was that the dogs barked at anything and everything, and so after a few days – or in some cases, a few hours – the owners stopped coming to see what the barking was about, rendering the animals all but useless except as a deterrent. But, on reflection, I supposed that sometimes that was enough.

Not this time, however; I'd not been deterred, and now I was on Pablo Pineda's front porch, knocking hard on the screen door as Kane played with the pit bull in the yard.

I retrieved the collapsible baton from my cargo pocket, holding it close against my thigh, tucked out of the way. When extended it measured a satisfying twenty-one inches, yet collapsed down to just nine inches of rubberized handle, making it eminently concealable against the rear of my forearm. There were larger models on the market, all the way up to thirty-two inches or more; but they were harder to conceal, and a bit of overkill. With good technique, there wasn't much this little baby couldn't do.

I could hear music coming from inside, now the pit bull's barking had subsided, and knew there was a chance that at least *someone* was in.

And then I heard shouts coming from inside, someone making their way to the door; and from the deep bass and aggressive tone, I guessed it wasn't Noemi.

Moments later the door was wrenched open by a big Latino, a can of beer in one hand and a baseball bat in the other. He was taller than me, and muscular, although some of it had turned to fat – presumably due to the beer. He was wearing only a pair of utility pants, his bare chest and arms covered in tattoos. A quick check showed that none were gang-related but – combined with his physique and the look of barely concealed rage on his lined and scarred face – the overall image was pretty fearsome.

Luckily though, I'd long since learned that appearances weren't everything. For all his ferocious bearing, he was out of shape and already half-drunk. A great role-model for his daughter.

His anger, however, seemed more directed toward his dog than me. "Hey!" he called out, looking over my shoulder. "*Puto perro!*" he spat. "What the fuck you doin', you lousy fuckin' dog?"

He took a swig of beer and turned disgustedly away from the pit bull to look at me. "So who the fuck are you?"

Before I could answer, there was a burst of Spanish from inside the house – another man, similar in age and tone to the man in front of me – and then the man at the door turned and yelled back. My Spanish wasn't fluent, but it was good enough; I think it went along the lines of, *Shut up, it's nobody, mind your own fucking business.* Nice.

"So *mano*," he said, addressing me again but this time gesturing toward me with the baseball bat. "Who the fuck are you, and what the fuck do you want?"

I could see out of the corner of my eye that Kane was checking us out, just in case he had to act; which was more than could be said for the pit bull, which was rolling around the yard on its back, blissfully unaware of the danger his owner might be in.

"I'm a reporter," I said, "following up a story from a few years back."

He looked at me and laughed. "You don' look like no reporter I ever fuckin' seen."

I supposed he was right, too – with work pants and a t-shirt, I might have been the scruffiest reporter ever. But it was one of the safer occupations to open with – he'd be unlikely to hit me with the bat, just in case.

He gestured with the bat toward me, then the gate. "But whoever you are, I got nothing to say to you. Now get the fuck off my property, before I fuck you up."

Well, I thought to myself, this wasn't going well; Plan B might be just around the corner. But in fairness, Plan B was where my real talents lay in any case.

"It's not really you I need to speak to anyway," I said, undeterred. "It's your daughter, Noemi. Is she in?"

The anger flashed in his eyes again. "What the fuck you want her for, homes?" He stepped forward off the porch, closing the distance. "Who the fuck *are* you?" He looked behind him. "Hey mano," he shouted to his friend inside, "s*alir aquí!*"

Get out here, he'd said, and I knew the interview was almost at an end; he'd attack when his friend arrived.

I nodded my head in acquiescence, let him think I was submitting and leaving; and then I unleashed my left hand, the metal baton extending from its collapsed position as it arced through the air.

With the whip-like action of my arm, the baton reached full extension just as it neared Pablo's head. The impact was like an explosion and the man's eyes went dull instantly, out cold before his big body hit the floor.

In the next instant I was leaping over the unconscious Pablo, checking who was coming along the hallway in the house beyond.

The man I saw charging down the hall was shorter than Pablo but stockier, more muscular, with a thick beard and a sweat-stained bandana.

And in his hand was a gun.

Chapter Seven

The most important thing in a fight is aggression, plain and simple. You can know all the fancy martial arts tricks in the world, but if you pussy-foot around with them, you're still going to be in a world of hurt if you try them out in the real world.

Speed and aggression win fights, period.

With that in mind, I sprinted toward the man with the gun, travelling fast toward the danger, my baton primed as he started to raise the snub-nosed .38 revolver toward me.

I let fly with the baton at just the right moment, slamming it down hard; heard the satisfying *crack* as the steel tip broke the radius bone of the man's forearm instants later. The gun fell harmlessly to the floor, followed by Pablo's friend, whose screams filled the narrow hallway.

I rushed in, placing the extended baton through my belt and drawing my knife. I crouched down over the crying man, put the knife to his throat as I'd done to Emilio earlier that very morning.

"Is there anyone else in the house?" I whispered, but the man was in too much pain to talk; and so I grabbed his head, turned his face to mine so that he could see me. "Nod if you understand me," I said, and he managed a single nod. "Good. Now, is anyone else in the house?" A shake of the head. "Juan?" A shake. "Noemi?" Another shake. "Okay," I said, before retrieving the revolver from the floor and crashing it into his head, right behind the ear. No sense leaving him awake; he'd recover from the initial shock sooner or later, and could be trouble. Asleep, we'd both be happy.

I tied him up with his own bandana, securing his wrists behind his back; if he woke up while I was still there, any movement he made would cause excruciating pain. I realized that might make him scream again, and so pulled a dirty sock from his foot and shoved it into his mouth. I hadn't had time to ask him if he was okay breathing through his nose, but I guessed we'd just have to take the chance.

I pocketed the gun and the knife, left the man in the hallway, and strode back to Pablo at the front door.

The pit bull seemed to have ignored the whole thing, but I was glad to see that Kane was still keeping a wary eye on the proceedings.

Pablo was still unconscious from the blow with the baton, and I had to drag his heavy, sweaty body back into the house; not an easy job, and certainly not one that I enjoyed. But it had to be done, and that was that.

I secured Pablo to a kitchen chair, hands bound behind the chair back, ankles strapped to the chair legs. I shoved a sock in his mouth, and decided to check the rest of the house while he recovered. His friend had told me there was nobody else, but there was nothing like checking for yourself if you were slightly paranoid.

The search took just a few minutes, and the man had been right; there was nobody else there.

The rest of the house was like the hallway and the kitchen – a mess. Downstairs there was just a living room, where Pablo and his friend had obviously been drinking. Music still blared from an old-school ghetto blaster, positioned on the frame of an old glass coffee table which had long since lost its glass. The TV was showing a rerun of last night's game, a playoff between the Dolphins and the Jets. I'd watched it live the night before in Herman's Bar on Dupont; it was nothing to write home about. Pizza boxes lay everywhere, and cigarette ends littered the room; ash trays were nowhere to be seen.

Upstairs, the bathroom and main bedroom were little better; I was surprised Pablo had never set fire to his mattress, the amount of butts that were lying everywhere. The only other room up there obviously belonged to a girl, which must have meant that the son – Juan – didn't live there anymore, if he ever had.

I was pleased to discover – from notebooks and various other paraphernalia – that the girl's room was

Noemi's, which meant that the girl still lived here, at least.

Which, I realized, might meant that she could be back at any moment. I didn't know if she was at school, if she worked, or if she'd just been out the night before and hadn't made it home yet. But if she was to enter her house to find a man lying tied up on the hallway floor, and her dad bound to a kitchen chair, it might be hard getting her to trust me.

And so I went back downstairs to wait for her, dragging the unconscious body of Pablo's friend into the kitchen so that – if Noemi did stroll in – it wouldn't be the first thing she saw.

I checked the man's pulse, pleased to see it was still there, thumping away happily. I saw that Pablo was awake now, watching me through droopy eyes.

"It's okay," I assured him, "he's still alive." I stood, and approached him. "And if you want me to be able to say the same about you in the next ten minutes, then I guess you're going to have to start answering some of my questions."

Yes, I decided, I was definitely a Plan B kind of guy.

Chapter Eight

To be fair to Pablo, he didn't talk; he might have called Noemi "a little slut" and "a fucking whore", but at least he didn't betray his own daughter by telling me where she was, or when she might be back. All credit to him, I thought.

But then again, he'd had it easy; I was never going to beat or torture the information out of him, I'd hoped the mere threat would be enough. I was bluffing, and he'd called it.

Hitting the man with the baton was one thing – it was simple self-defense. But tying someone up and hurting them was something else again, especially if they hadn't done anything wrong. And Pablo Pineda – as far as I was aware – had done nothing wrong.

And so after he refused to answer my questions, I merely left him sitting there with the sock in his mouth as I crashed onto the sofa to wait for Noemi to return home. I'd wait a few hours and see what happened, then readdress my strategy if she didn't turn up.

Fate was kind to me though, and after only one painful hour of daytime TV, Kane's playful yapping warned me that someone was coming.

I immediately leaped to my feet and checked through the living room window, careful to keep out of sight.

A girl, mid- to late-teens, dressed for a night on the town and now more than a little worse for wear.

Noemi.

She paused as she entered the yard, confused to see Kane there but delighted as he played his role well and brushed up against her, eliciting a rub under his chin. He dropped to the ground, rolled over, and encouraged her to tickle his belly, which she did.

It was then that I ran around to the front door and pushed it open, striding out confidently while looking over my shoulder. "I will do," I shouted back to the imaginary person in the hallway, "you too. Thanks very much!"

I turned forward, acted surprised to see Noemi there.

"Oh," I said, "I'm sorry, you must be Mr. Pineda's daughter, Noemi."

I extended my hand, and she rose to her feet and took it, her expression quizzical.

"And you are . . ." she said with a raised eyebrow.

"Sorry, sorry," I said, releasing her hand, "I'm Brad

Ranson. You've met Kane already, I see." I smiled at her in the most friendly way I knew how.

"But who *are* you?" she asked, and I could see the other question hidden behind the first – *and why hasn't my dad beaten you up?*

"I'm a private investigator," I said, trying something else seeing as how the reporter trick had done me no good. "And it wasn't your father I came here to see, it was you. I represent the family of someone you used to know."

Her head hung down on her chest for a few moments before she met my eye again. "Elena?" she asked me, and I nodded. "Ah, shit." She paused, looked at her house, thinking. "Can we go somewhere else to talk?" she asked.

I nodded my head, smiling again. "It wouldn't please me more," I said, taking her arm gently and guiding her away from the house with the two tied up men hidden within. "Honestly, it wouldn't please me more."

Fifteen minutes later we were entering a nice little place called Caffe Dolce, up on Victoria Avenue. It had paninis, salads and croissants – not the usual fare for this area, stuffed full as it was with burrito bars and taco delis, and I approved the choice. It looked to have some promising coffees too.

We'd not spoken for most of the journey, and I was surprised that Noemi didn't ask why we were walking, why I didn't have a car; most people did.

Caffe Dolce was her suggestion; she said they did great food, but I was surprised she didn't pick something closer – the whole neighborhood was filled with coffee shops and fast food joints.

But as we entered, and the staff members all greeted Noemi by name, it became obvious; she worked here, and wanted a familiar environment in which to meet an unfamiliar man. A smart move.

"Hey-hey, good lookin'," a young man said from behind the deli counter. "Good night last night?"

Noemi smiled. "The best," she said. "You?"

The young man shook his head. "Stayed in *aaaaalll* night long," he said. "Needed the rest after the weekend. Man, I don't know how you do it."

"Practice," Noemi said with a laugh, then gestured over to a table in the corner. "We'll be over there, okay?"

The look in her eye said it all – *please keep an eye on us.*

"Sure thing," the young man said with a smile, while at the same time casting a suspicious look my way.

We took a seat, and as I picked up a menu, Noemi – so silent on the journey here – got started straight away. "So tell me," she said, "how did you get out of my house without my *papá* doin' a number on your head with his bat?"

I sat back in my chair, observing her. What should I tell her? What sort of girl was she? A party girl, sure, but she was bright; I thought she might already have her own suspicions, and I wanted her to trust me. Should I

52

be honest?

What the hell, I figured. *Why not?*

"He tried," I said. "I clocked him with a night stick." Before she could react, I opened my hands, palms out. "It was self-defense," I said, "and he's okay, he's just sleeping it off. But I don't want to lie to you, Noemi. I want you to trust me."

"You beat up my dad and you want me to *trust* you?" she asked, eyes wide with incredulity.

Had I misread her? Was this conversation going to be over before it had even started?

But then she smiled, and I could see she'd been teasing me. "Ha," she said, "the bastard probably deserved it anyway. He's a pig. Was he alone?"

"He was with a friend," I said, "short stocky guy. Had a gun."

She looked worried. "And what did you do to *him?*"

"The same thing," I said. "They're both asleep in the kitchen right now."

She laughed again, long and loud. "Oh, that's priceless," she said. "Priceless. His friend, Manuel, he fancies himself as a real *esse*, you know, a real gangster. But he's full of shit, just like my dad. They just get drunk and watch football, just like the rest of their lame-ass friends."

I was beginning to understand why Noemi had been so willing to come with me; whatever I was offering, it would probably be better than a morning at home.

We decided that Noemi could order for me, and she went off to speak to the young man at the counter. She came back with a lemongrass tea for herself, and a Vietnamese coffee for me – dried chicory with sweetened condensed milk. Not my usual, but it was pretty damned good; it pays to keep an open mind, I guess. She took a bowl of water out to Kane as well, who was waiting patiently outside, and I appreciated the gesture.

"So," she said, sipping from her cup, "what do you wanna know, mano? Police asked me a bunch of questions three years ago, and I don' think the answers helped 'em much."

"What I want to know, Noemi," I said, placing my own cup down on the table in front of me, "is the name of the boy Elena was meeting on the other side of the bridge."

It was a shot in the dark, but it was a numbers game – if there was a demonstrable change in a teenager's behavior, it was almost certainly connected to the opposite sex. I'd seen it many times in this line of work, and I was just playing the odds.

There was a brief flicker in Noemi's eyes, and I knew I'd been barking up the right tree. She tried to hide it, but it was too late.

"You don' know *nuthin'*," she said. "There was no boyfriend, least not that I know of."

"I didn't say *boyfriend*," I argued, "I just said *boy*. And I think that you know a hell of a lot more than you make out, and a whole lot more than you told the

54

police. Look," I said, settling back in my chair and trying to sound reasonable, "Elena's parents are pressuring the police to open up the books on this again, and they think *you* were the one that went across to Nuevo Laredo with her."

"That's bullshit!" Noemi exploded, and I noticed the young man looking across at us from behind the counter. I hoped for his sake that he would decide to mind his own business. "I didn't go with her!"

"So she *did* go," I pressured, glad that things were opening up ever so slowly. Before this, I couldn't even be sure that Elena had even crossed the border.

"I . . ." Noemi's shoulders sagged as she looked at me. I could see the thought of a police investigation was niggling at her. "I . . ."

"It's okay," I said. "Look – if I can find out what happened to Elena, the police won't become involved, it'll just stay a private matter between me and her parents. I'm just one man, your name won't be mentioned anywhere. But if I don't find out anything, then I'll have to go back and say I've failed, and they'll try the Laredo PD again, maybe even the FBI. They're literally at the breaking point. So listen. You help me, you'll stay clean. Don't, and" – I held up my hands apologetically – "I won't be able to help *you*. Besides, don't you want to find out what happened to her yourself? I thought she was your friend?"

"She *was* my friend," Noemi shot back. "And yeah, we did go across the bridge a few times."

A few times? Interesting. "You were the one who

encouraged her?"

"Maybe," she said. "Maybe I was. But the night she went missing, I wasn't with her, I swear. She went without me."

I could piece together the rest of the tale by the look in her eyes – betrayal and deceit, wounds from the past being opened up again. The boy across the river was someone *Noemi* liked, and that Elena was going to meet behind her back.

"To see the boy?" I coaxed, and Noemi nodded her head sadly.

"Bitch," she said, still angry after all those years. "I take her over there, get her introduced, get her into the clubs, you know? Then she goes and takes Santiago from me, I mean right out from under my nose, you know?" She shook her head, as if she still couldn't believe it. "I mean, what was she doing? What the hell was she doing? She was supposed to be a *friend*, and she did that shit to me."

I sipped slowly at the chicory coffee as I listened to her, various scenarios playing across my mind. The first was that Noemi might be responsible for Elena's disappearance in some way. In a fit of jealous rage, did she suggest to one of the cartels that Elena was ripe for the plucking? Did she set up the kidnap? Or did she actually kill Elena herself, then hide the body?

I had another name to go on now, too – Santiago. Who was he? Was he still in the picture, over in Nuevo Laredo?

There were so many questions, and I hoped Noemi

would continue to answer them.

"Did you kill her?" I asked, completely deadpan. No point beating around the bush, right?

She looked at me as if I was crazy, and I studied her expression as she did so; and then she burst out laughing, nearly falling off her chair.

"Me?" she gasped, after regaining some semblance of control over herself. "Me? I don' even step on flies man, I don' be hurtin' nobody. Did I kill her? *Shit*. If that's the best you got, you've got problems, mano."

I smiled at her. "I guess you're right," I said. "But when I tell the police what you've told me, you'll start to have some pretty serious problems too. Because they'll start asking the same questions I am. Like, *did you kill her?*"

"No man," she said, eyes wide, taken aback by the force of my last question. "No way, I'd never do that man, never."

"Okay," I said, "so why don't you lead me through things, step by step?"

She looked at me, then nodded her head. "Okay mano," she said, "okay. When do you want me to start?"

"Why not start with your first visit to Nuevo Laredo, and we'll go from there?"

She took a deep breath, got control of herself, and began her tale.

CHAPTER NINE

Noemi had joined the same high school as Elena, and they'd become friends within days of knowing each other; Noemi's wild, party-child nature must have awakened some inner desire in Elena to seek out some excitement in her own life.

Noemi had heard about the parties that occurred over the river, how young girls were allowed into clubs, and she encouraged Elena to speak to her family about it over in Nuevo Laredo. Elena did as she was asked, and found a willing cousin to help them.

And so it was that Mateo Ramirez – a twenty-year-old cousin of Elena's on her mother's side – had driven across to Laredo one night, picked them up and driven back to Mexico, where he and his friends had taken them into Nuevo Laredo's downtown party zone. And to hear Noemi tell it, it had been everything it had been

58

cracked up to be – drugs and drink everywhere, and nobody too young to party all night.

There was a gang presence, sure; they saw violence in the clubs, on the streets, but that in some ways was another part of the thrill, the excitement. It was the feeling that they were in forbidden territory, completely alien to them. And when Mateo and his friends had demanded sex with the teenage girls, they had complied readily; their judgement was clouded by alcohol and drugs, but also by their hormones and the added excitement of being found attractive by older boys, men. They hadn't seen anything wrong with it, and Noemi had eventually become involved with a young man called Santiago Alvarado.

Santiago was a low-level dealer for a small gang that worked for Los Zetas, the number one cartel in the area after a series of battles with the Gulf and Sinaloa cartels. He was twenty-one, handsome, and – as far as Elena and Noemi could see – rich.

Although Noemi had been with him first, Elena had also fallen for him hard, and when Noemi found out they'd argued furiously. Elena claimed to have already slept with him, but Noemi hadn't believed it at the time.

But then one evening, when Mateo hadn't come for her, Noemi discovered that he'd already picked up Elena and taken her across to meet Santiago.

After that, nobody had ever seen Elena again; and it was also clear that Noemi was no longer welcome down there. With no family of her own in Mexico, border crossings would have been more problematic anyway, and so her weekend visits came to an end.

"Mateo never said anything to the police?" I asked Noemi, and she shook her head.

"Not that I know of, no. Nobody says anything to the police in Mexico, don' you know that?"

"And Elena's parents didn't know about what Mateo had been doing?"

"I don' know," Noemi said, "but I guess not, otherwise they would have told you, huh?"

It was true, I supposed; they would have. "And why didn't you say anything? If you'd fingered Santiago, you could have got your own back."

"And been killed for it," Noemi said matter-of-factly. "They got no problems sending their *sicarios* north of the border, you know? Santiago was a small-time dealer, but he was connected, and you don' go messin' with that. It wouldn't have been just me either – they would have killed my entire family."

"So why tell me?"

"I don' know . . . I guess a part of it is that I *do* trust you, crazy as it sounds. You might be . . . more *subtle* than the police, I don' think you'll be involving the law or taking anything to court, am I right?"

I nodded my head. "You're right," I said. "Although maybe not so much about the *subtle* part."

"Ha," she said, "that's fair enough, mano. But either way, I don' think you'll be telling anyone about me. And I guess I *do* feel bad about what happened to her. At the time, I wished she was dead, you know? Or maybe worse, maybe one of their whores or somethin', I don' know. I guess you must think I'm a real bitch, but I was young, and she'd hurt me, and I guess I dealt with it like a kid. And then time passed, and she wasn't found, and . . . I don' know . . . I guess I thought it was over. But if she's still alive . . . and you find her . . . I'd like to tell her I'm sorry."

I put my hand on hers across the table and held her gaze. "I promise you," I said earnestly, "I will do everything in my power to give you that opportunity."

So phase one was over; I had two names, Mateo and Santiago, and I just knew they would have some of the answers I was looking for.

It was time to move on to Mexico.

PART TWO

CHAPTER ONE

I crossed the border with one of the fake IDs I carry with me. I was wanted in a number of states, so I used a variety of different identities when travelling. This was the first time I was moving outside the United States though, and I was pleased that I was let through with no more than a cursory glance at the fake passport.

I would have needed all sorts of paperwork to take Kane with me though and so – reluctantly – I had to leave him in the hands of Emilio and Camila. They seemed like good people though, and I was sure he'd be fine until I got back.

I was carrying a day sack with me – put together from the side pouches of my main rucksack – along with a jacket and a walking stick. I'd left a lot of my gear behind, including my weapons; it just wasn't worth getting stopped at the border.

That being said, the walking stick wasn't exactly as harmless as it looked. It was basically a four-foot long hardwood pole with a leather strap at the top; perfect as a weapon in itself, it could also separate in the middle to give me two perfectly sized *Escrima* sticks.

Escrima, also called *Arnis* or *Kali*, is a Philippine martial art which emphasizes combat with sticks, knives and other bladed weapons. If the US has a "gun culture", then the Philippines definitely has a "knife culture"; whereas most Western blade arts have become extinct, those of the Philippines are alive and thriving. Filipinos are even referred to as *chad ra oles* by the nearby Palau islanders – "the people of the knife". Legend has it that the famous Colt M1911 with its man-stopping .45 ACP round was developed after a Moro tribesman decapitated a US serviceman during the Philippine-American War at the turn of the nineteenth century – even after the soldier had emptied his .38 revolver into him.

Sticks are also very important to the art, and experts practice continually with either the single stick, or double sticks – typically twenty-six inch lengths of rattan.

I'd been involved in the art for many years myself – hence my love of the collapsible baton as a concealable weapon. Before my selection for the Regimental Recon Detachment, I'd been my unit's unarmed combat instructor, and – in addition to the main curriculum of US Army Combatives, which was heavily based on Gracie Jiujitsu – we'd mixed in a lot of other things, including Muay Thai, freestyle wrestling, boxing and various other arts. Knife work had been important too, but it was only when I was posted to the RRD that I became exposed to the Filipino arts, which changed my entire outlook.

One of my close friends was Manuel Lapada, the son of Filipino immigrants and a master of Escrima, in all its aspects – sticks, knives, kicking, punching, locking, throwing and grappling. He introduced me to it, and I trained with him intensively, even accompanying him on trips home to the Philippines where I met his family; the older guys were all grandmasters, and had a wealth of scars from past duels, where they'd perfected their technique in the most realistic conditions available – actual fights. The fact that they were all still alive had told me a lot.

Our operational experience also tainted what I had learned – and taught – as a combatives instructor; and so Manuel and I had started up a program of brutally efficient armed and unarmed combatives training which combined the different aspects of Escrima with the deadly, back-to-basics tactics of World War II commando fighting methods, which I'd also been researching. It wasn't regulated or authorized, but it was damned effective.

The bottom line, of course, was that the walking stick I carried was more dangerous in my hands than a machine pistol in the hands of most people. That being said though, I hoped I wouldn't have to prove it; I believed in the easy life if at all possible, and antagonizing the local cartels was something I would try and avoid at all costs.

I'd not asked Emilio to call ahead for me to arrange a meeting with Mateo – I didn't want the cousin to be alerted to my visit, to maybe panic and run. I'd asked Emilio about his family members south of the border though, and taken careful note when he came on to Mateo; the guy was still alive it seemed, and still living in Nuevo Laredo. It wasn't too much of a surprise; unless they joined the military, most people from neighborhoods like that tended to stay there. I took note of all the addresses he had for them, and told him not to let anyone know I was coming.

As I cleared the Gateway to the Americas International Bridge, stepping foot onto Mexican soil for the first time in years, I breathed in deeply, trying to acclimatize myself to the new setting. There might be just a river separating them, but Nuevo Laredo was going to be a whole other world to its northern twin, I could sense that straight away.

And I could only hope that somewhere, in that world, I would be able to find a young woman called Elena Rosales.

CHAPTER TWO

Nuevo Laredo was hot, dusty and dirty; the air was thick and powerful, you could feel the atmosphere all around you, working its way into your bones.

Most of the people here were Latino and Hispanic, but I didn't feel particularly out of place – there was such a streaming mass of humanity coming across the border in both directions that I was just one more, hidden in the onslaught of busy human flesh. Nobody paid me any attention at all.

That changed before long however, when I steered away from the main tourist traps and places of work and headed toward the more residential districts, my walking stick click-clacking along with me as I went.

Most of Emilio's family lived west of the Avenue César López de Lara, the main road south through the city. Apparently Mateo still lived there too, though further north than his parents nowadays, up on Calle Indepencia – which was where I was now headed.

If I'd still been in the military, I would have spent time doing a full-blown reconnaissance of the city, starting off with a complete intel dump on the place – crime stats, bad neighborhoods, street layout, police presence, no-go areas, drug hotspots, the whole shebang – before I'd even set foot there. Then there would static and mobile surveillance on my targets before I made a move, including weeks – and possibly even months – of groundwork. But I just didn't have the patience for it anymore, nor the desire to operate that way. That phase of my life, full of meticulous planning and rehearsal, was over. Now I just liked to work off-the-cuff; rattle some cages and see what happened. It was definitely more me.

As it turned out, I hadn't even rattled any cages before something happened. I'd come off the bridge and continued south onto Leandro Valle, passing business after business on the busy street – garages, pharmacies, doctors' and dentists' offices, visa bureaus, everything a good border town needed. Some were run-down, others looked pretty new, but the overall impression was still that of a Wild West frontier town, with violence just around any corner.

Turning right onto Belden, I kept to the broken sidewalk to avoid the rush of cars down the narrow street. I passed a hospital and some parking lots, and even though I'd only been walking for twenty minutes, the atmosphere was already changing and I was starting to see the real Nuevo Laredo. Concrete walls separated plots of land, plasterwork crumbling after years of neglect; colonial-era buildings which might have once been pretty were now living on borrowed time, façades worn and battered; seedy basement bars lay nestled underneath dilapidated grocery and tobacco stores, the sky above almost blocked out by fantastic patterns of interwoven electricity cables, stretching from one rooftop to the next in never-ending cobwebs. It all seemed destined for the developer's wrecking ball; but everyone here knew that the developers were never coming.

The people, too, were changing as I moved west; young boys acted as lookouts on street corners, young men wandered restlessly from stoop to stoop, bulges underneath their baggy basketball shirts hinting at concealed weapons that weren't really concealed, young women wearing next to nothing already plying their trade on the adjacent streets, even at this hour of the day.

I turned south again, trotted down the Avenue Riva Palacio, then crossed the Avenue César López de Lara along Calle de Mier, which ran underneath the main road with its thunderous traffic.

There was a sidewalk on either side of Riva, with steps running beneath, and I took the left hand side so that I could see the traffic coming toward me. I'd already checked that there was nobody on foot, waiting in the shadows.

By the time I was halfway along the underpass, however, things started to rapidly change. First of all, there was a car coming up behind me on the opposite side of the road; then I sensed it swerve across, heard its brakes; and then it was right beside me, before I'd had time to run. Its windows were down, *Ranchera* music blasting out from the interior.

I held my ground, a part of me curious to see what would happen; I was about to get an introduction to Mexico, and I didn't want to be impolite.

The driver kept looking ahead, keeping his eye out for the police. But behind him, out of the rear passenger window, I saw a man leaning toward me with a smile.

"*Norte Americano?*" he asked, and I nodded my head, which elicited a wider smile. I'd counted five men in the car, two up front and three in the rear; I didn't smile back. "I can help you, maybe, yeah?" the man said, golden teeth gleaming.

"Help me how?" I asked, already calculating angles of attack.

"Your backpack looks heavy," he sniffed. "Hot day like this. Hand it over, we'll take it. Make it easier to walk. Your wallet too *gringo*, eh?"

This time I did smile. "That's very kind of you," I said, and I could see my response had confused the man. I could see also that his partners were busily scouting the surrounding roads, nervous – it was already taking too long. "But I'm afraid my answer will have to be a big 'fuck you', okay?"

There was a look of blank disbelief on the man's face for a moment; but then he started reacting, shouting in Spanish to his cohorts, raising his hand out of the window toward me.

But I was already reacting myself, forcing the tip of my walking stick through the open window and catching the man straight in the eyeball with a sharp thrust that made him scream out in pain, the gun dropping somewhere to the floor of the car.

His friends were out now, racing around to me; with the driver still at the wheel, that left three of them – two with flick knives, one with a two-foot long machete.

The two from the rear got to me first, but as they rounded the car I was already swinging the wooden pole toward them; I caught the first man on the side of the neck as he cleared the trunk, stunning him. I immediately pulled the stick back then fired it out in a forward thrust toward the next man, catching him high in the chest. He fell back into the street, dropping his knife and then screaming as he saw the van that was traveling toward him, unable to stop in time. It caught him on the hip and spun him wildly out into the street behind until he fell, broken, to the ground. The van never even stopped.

The man I'd caught in the neck was recovering, maybe thinking of coming for me again; I discouraged him by smashing the hardwood staff right over his head, dropping him unconscious to the floor.

The man in the car was still screaming over his popped eyeball, frantically searching the car floor, half-blind, for his pistol.

And then the third man was finally there on the

sidewalk beside me, chopping down heavily toward my head with the machete. I moved in to the attack, dropping my staff as I blocked his arm with my own, following through with my other hand to trap his arm completely, holding it in a figure-four around his wrist. With a sudden jerk, I wrenched downwards, breaking the arm at the shoulder and driving him to the concrete sidewalk. The machete left his hand as the shoulder broke, and I followed him down with a knee to the exposed floating ribs, my weight crushing him and breaking a few of them. I kicked the machete underneath the car, then noticed that the man in the car had finally found his gun and was once more pushing it out of the window toward me.

I moved instantly, deflecting the gun to the side; it went off, the round hitting the underpass wall, the noise tremendously loud in the confined space. At the same time I lashed out with my hand, tip of my thumb braced against my bunched knuckles. It hit the target squarely, right in the man's *other* eye, and he cried out in pain once again; and once again, he dropped the gun, this time outside the car; and then he was screaming at the driver in Spanish, and the car pulled away from the curb and hightailed it out of there, motor gunning at dangerously high revs.

I looked around at the three men left behind; all were still out of it, especially the one who'd been hit by the van.

I simply loosened my shoulders, rolled my neck, and bent down to pick up my walking stick. I picked up the gun too, and pocketed it.

With a welcome to Mexico like this, I was sure it wouldn't be long before I'd be needing it.

CHAPTER THREE

I saw Mateo Ramirez for the first time at just after four o'clock that afternoon.

He was coming out of his dilapidated single-story home, dressed in baggy pants which barely contained a heaving gut, along with the ubiquitous oversized basketball shirt. He looked older than his twenty-three years; Emilio had shown me a picture of him as a normal-looking seventeen year old kid, and the years hadn't been kind to him. His rough face was hidden behind several days of stubble and his greasy hair was slicked back in a ponytail; all in all, I could well imagine him as someone willing to pass around his thirteen-year-old Norte Americano cousin to his buddies.

He lit up a joint as he stood on the sidewalk, obviously waiting for his ride to come and pick him up.

There was a convenience store directly opposite,

covered in large, broken advertisements for Coca Cola and Tecate beer. I'd sauntered over and was reading these assorted signs which decorated the exterior, pretending to decipher them as I watched Mateo across the street.

Far from being a regular gangbanger's car, what pulled up instead was a purple VW Beetle; I could still hear the ranchero music playing inside though. It was driven by a heavy-set guy right around the same age as Mateo, who threw the passenger side door open and began shouting at his friend to get in; apparently they were going to be late for something.

They didn't know the half of it, I thought darkly.

Mateo got in, and I set off from the stoop of the convenience store, ambling across the road casually. I didn't have a car of my own with which to follow him, and so I decided to take the bull by the horns and act while he was already in sight.

As the passenger door closed, I increased my speed, matching it just right so that I was pulling open the rear door and getting in just as the car pulled out into the street. There was a look of shock on the driver's face as he turned in his seat, even more so when he saw the gun I had pointed at the back of Mateo's head. It was the weapon I'd taken from the man who'd recently attacked me; another .38 revolver like the one Pablo's friend had tried to use, back on the other side of the river.

"Keep driving," I said, "or your friend here will be decorating your windshield with his brains."

Mateo, sensibly, kept looking forward, all too aware of the cold barrel which rested just above his ponytail; and then his friend got the message and got his eyes forward too, carrying on driving just as I'd asked.

"What the fuck you want, mano?" the driver breathed, almost too scared to talk but getting the words out anyway.

"I want to have a word with your friend Mateo here," I said. "And you're just going to drive us around until I'm finished."

"Then you'll kill us!" the driver whispered, already puling the car over to the side of the road. With my free hand I banged my walking staff into the back of his head, just to get his mind back on what he should be doing.

"Don't even think about stopping the car," I warned him, "or I *will* kill you both, here and now."

The driver nodded slowly and got the car back straight. "Where you wanna go man?" he asked, and I gave him a quick set of directions. They weren't for any destination in particular, they were just so that he didn't decide to drive me into the middle of a gangbangers' convention with a bunch of his best friends; he seemed harmless enough, but you could never tell.

"You've been quiet there," I said to Mateo. "I hope you're able to say something, or this will be a real short trip for all of us."

"Okay mano," he managed, "it's just hard to fuckin' think with a gun at your head, you know?"

Actually I *did* know, but this wasn't a time to be

swapping war stories. "It's amazing what you can accomplish if you try," I said pleasantly.

"Yeah man, I'll try, okay? I'll fuckin' try. What do you want?"

"I want to see what you can remember about a little thirteen-year-old girl called Elena Rosales. You probably remember her – she was your cousin, you pimped her out to your buddies, then you drove her over here the night she went missing."

There was a pause from the front seat, then I saw Mateo's shoulders slump.

"Aw, *shit*," was all he could manage.

But I knew there would be more.

CHAPTER FOUR

We'd been driving around the alternatingly empty or terribly congested streets of Nuevo Laredo for over an hour, and I'd learned plenty.

Mateo had first denied having anything to do with his cousin, but after a bit of persuasion – involving the percussive use of the revolver butt on his pitted, stubbled face – he had admitted to much of what Noemi had told me.

He had helped bring the girls across in his car, and they'd had a great time in the town's party zones, most notably a local nightclub called Eclipse – apparently a prime location for underage kids from over the river.

Unfortunately, the club was also a hangout for various cartel hoodlums – and Santiago Alvarado was one of them. Mateo denied any involvement with the local gangs, and from my current experience with him and his friend, I was of a mind to believe him; but the girls apparently *had* become involved, both seeking the attentions of Santiago.

He'd gone with Noemi first, and then with Elena; the night Elena had gone missing, Mateo had been working on the instructions of Santiago, who'd told him to bring her across alone, and drop her off outside Eclipse to wait for him.

Mateo had done so – reluctantly, to hear him tell it – and had hightailed it out of there, not willing to get caught up in whatever Santiago had wanted with her. It clashed slightly with his claim that he had no gang affiliations, but just because he wasn't a part of the cartels didn't mean that he wouldn't do what they told him – to have told Santiago "no" would have been the same as signing his own death warrant.

I loathed Mateo for the way he had used the two young girls, found his proclivities disgusting and offensive; but it was also clear that he had no real involvement in organized crime himself, was just a party boy like Noemi was a party girl. Innocent, as far as he could be.

Still, I was tempted to shoot him; he'd brought his teenage cousin into Mexico for the sexual pleasure of his buddies, maybe even himself. He was the scum of the earth, but – on balance – I decided that killing him might just bring added complications. I wasn't a murderer, after all.

Santiago himself had risen another couple of rungs up the corporate ladder over the past three years, was now running his own little pack of street dealers; not in the big leagues just yet, but taking scraps from the table.

Mateo was less sure about Elena though, claiming he had never seen her since the night he had left her to meet Santiago outside Eclipse, that he had no idea what had become of her.

I wasn't sure whether I believed him – was his recalcitrance on the subject because he really didn't know, or just because he was more afraid of Santiago and the cartels than he was of me? If it was the latter, I couldn't really blame him – for all my bluster, I wouldn't cut off any body parts, whereas the cartels would be more than happy to do so.

"Where does Santiago hang out now?" I asked. "Still at Eclipse?"

"Nah, man," Mateo said. "That place done closed down now, man. Too many gunfights there, too many people dead, you know? No, he works his crew over in La Zona."

"La Zona?" I asked.

"Yeah, *La Zona de Tolerancia*, the zone of tolerance, sometimes called Boy's Town – it's a walled compound down off Calle Monterrey, full of brothels and bars, you know? It's perfect for Santiago, a real captive audience. And it's got its own police protection too, got a fuckin' substation of municipal cops there, you know? They leave the way clear for Santiago and his crew."

I nodded my head in thought. It made sense; Santiago worked for Z201, a sub-gang of the all-powerful Los Zetas cartel who owned pretty much all the vice operations in the city. If there were brothels there being protected by the police, Santiago's operation would receive equal backing.

I wondered, briefly, if Elena would be there; then I scratched the thought from my mind and focused my attention back on Mateo.

"Santiago there often?"

"Every might, man! Every night – he's a boss, he's gotta keep his eye on things, you know?"

Okay, I thought, *okay*; I had my next target.

I would make my way to Boy's Town that night and seek out Santiago Alvarado, see what he could tell me about the disappearance of Elena Rosales.

"Pull over here," I told Mateo's friend, who dutifully and eagerly did as I asked.

"You said you weren't gonna kill us, mano," he reminded me, his voice still breathless.

"And I won't," I said. "*Unless* you say anything to anybody about this. Don't forget," I said, tapping the snub-nose revolver against the back of Mateo's head, "I know where you live, as do my associates." I didn't have any associates of course, but Mateo didn't have to know that. I tapped the driver on the head next, making sure I had his attention.

"Show me your driver's license," I said, and watched as he slipped it reluctantly out of the sun visor. I studied it, then handed it back. "Okay," I said, "and now I know where *you* live, too. So please. Don't make me do anything I might regret."

The car was pulled over now, just outside the

Hospital San Jose on Sonora, near the center of town.

Without another word, I was out of the car and gone, leaving the two young men behind me both scared, and barely able to believe what had just happened to them.

I headed west toward a restaurant I'd seen as we'd driven past. El Papalote Taco and Grill – perfect for a hungry man. I'd not eaten for a long time, and it had been a busy day.

Would they warn Santiago? I asked myself as I walked along Sonora. It was fifty-fifty either way, but I didn't think they would; if they did, they would have to tell him how I knew how to find him, which would mean they would probably be killed as snitches. On the other hand, if they didn't tell him and Santiago got the better of me and I revealed who had told me, then their deaths would probably be much, much worse.

So it was still fifty-fifty, and I wouldn't know until later tonight.

But I wasn't one for worrying unduly, especially when I was hungry.

What would be, would be; if Santiago was ready and waiting for me, then so be it.

But right now, there was a plate full of tacos waiting with my name all over it.

CHAPTER FIVE

La Zona de Tolerancia was, without a doubt, one of the most depraved, depressing and desperate shitholes I had ever visited.

It was late night now and the place was filling up with characters of every sort. At least I wasn't too out of place here – many of my own citizens crossed the border expressly to use the services of "Boy's Town", and I was among plenty of Caucasian company.

Earlier that day – after eating my fill at El Papalote – I'd wandered over to the Avenue César López de Lara to find a hotel, just in case I had to stay here longer than I wanted to. I'd chosen the main drag as it was comparatively peaceful and well looked after. There was a strong police presence, with the Mexican military also being in evidence, and it therefore looked safe, as far as anywhere in Nuevo Laredo could be.

I found the Hotel Cólon Plaza not long after, just a short walk south. It looked reasonable, and so I'd gone in and taken a room for just over seven hundred pesos a night. One of the best hotels in the city for a little over forty dollars; maybe not everything here was as bad as I thought.

I'd had a shower, changed to fresh clothes from my day-sack, then rested up for a few hours. I could have done a recon of the area during daylight hours, but I hadn't wanted to draw attention to myself – and being one of the only people wandering through the walled-in streets before dark would definitely have marked me. The people there would have a sixth sense for things being out of place – if they wanted to survive more than a night or two, that is – and solo surveillance would have been a tough task.

I'd therefore chosen to get some rest before hitting the streets again; during combat operations, I'd learned to nap when the opportunity presented itself, as you never knew when it might do so again.

When I set off that night – delighted to learn that the Zone was only a few blocks directly west of the hotel – I decided to leave my wooden walking pole behind; it would make me stick out like a sore thumb, and I didn't want to attract attention too early on.

I also decided to leave the .38; if Mateo was right and there was a police presence, they might refuse me entry. Or even worse, I could end up in jail; and a Mexican jail was definitely somewhere I didn't want to be.

I didn't consider myself to be weaponless, however; within minutes of entering the Zone, I would have a bottle or a beer glass in my hand, and there were always plenty of weapons of opportunity available in bars, from ashtrays to chairs – the only limit was the imagination.

I'd come off the main road of Calle Monterrey at just past midnight, after passing by the crumbling wall which separated – barely – La Zona from the rest of the city. I'd had to pass through a military-style guard post on the way in – apparently a remnant of times past, as it was unmanned and in a state of near-ruin – and entered another world entirely.

A call from my right drew my attention to a uniformed cop however, and it became clear that the guardhouse – while looking like it hadn't been used in years – was actually still an active security point for the Zone.

The cop – dark and grim-faced – had been chatting to a young guy by the compound wall, in what looked to be something of a business meeting. But when he saw me, he broke off from what he was doing and approached.

He gave me a quick search, and I found myself grateful that I'd left my weapons behind in my hotel room.

"Been here before?" he asked in English and – up close now – I could see how sweat-stained his uniform was, how few teeth he had left, how he smelled of body odor and cigarettes.

I shook my head.

He was about to speak, then saw a taxi pull up outside the compound, three more white Americans getting out and stumbling over, already half-drunk.

"Wait," he told me, as he approached the men and searched them one by one; I guessed he couldn't be bothered repeating himself, and wanted to give us the bad news all together.

"Okay," he said when he was finished, "now listen. You boys be good, okay? You give no trouble, you get no trouble, you understand? Some of the people here can be … nasty," he said with a snigger, "know what I mean? Try not to upset them."

He gestured to his left, to what looked like an abandoned old-West jail; although on closer inspection, the metal bars were all new, and an attempt had been made to repaint it. And – over the cacophonous noise of the nearby bars – I could just make out the sounds of a boxing match being played on a TV somewhere inside; probably the cop's colleagues, and who knew how many there might be in there? Presumably, this was the substation of the municipal police that Mateo had mentioned. It looked in one hell of a state, but would do just as good a job of keeping a man locked up as any other cell block.

"And if we need to come and get you, if we need to sort things out, then there's a home waiting for you right there," he said. "And believe me, you don't want to end up in *there*."

He tried to smile then, but it came out more as a malicious leer. "Welcome to La Zona!" he exclaimed in mock happiness, hand sweeping out to the interior of the compound to usher us in.

I stumbled into the township with the three other Americans, but soon lost them as they made a run for the nearest brothel they could find – a nasty little shack called Los Amazonas.

The streets were teeming with people, many of them locals but with a fair amount of tourists mixed in there; touts were moving in and out of the crowds with flyers for popular bars, and a line of talk to entice people inside.

If the rest of Nuevo Laredo could at best be labelled as low-rent, I wasn't sure what term could be used to accurately describe the three block walled compound of La Zona. It was, literally, a city within the city – and one dedicated entirely to vice and depravity in all its forms.

The township was established in the sixties as an area to centralize Nuevo Laredo's bustling prostitution industry, mainly for the use of US soldiers. It had catered to millions of US citizens ever since, many of whom had crossed the border expressly to use its unrivalled services which – at its prime – had even included nightly "donkey shows". I'd heard that the days of the donkey had been numbered more recently, however, and found myself being grateful for small mercies.

If the guard post and police station were showing signs of ruin, it was only indicative of the rest of the compound itself. Cartel violence in the city had driven

US customers away in droves, and many of the buildings within the Zone were empty, abandoned and almost literally falling down. But since Los Zetas had all but won the local drug wars, and the horrific violence was starting to settle down to the merely abhorrent, some of the bars and brothels were starting to regain a little of their past sparkle.

I spotted a tout as I wandered the streets, and let myself drift into a position where I could be targeted; if I wanted information, I could spend hours drifting from brothel to bar and back to brothel but – as impatient as I was – I knew there was a quicker way.

"Hey mano," the young kid said, with a smile that seemed almost genuine, "how you doin' tonight? You American, right? Right, course you are, no sweat, right? Right?"

He was in my face now, up close and still grinning from ear to ear. "Right," I replied, and the kid's grin spread even wider.

"You go in here, yeah?" he said, pointing to a nearby den called Bar Oasis – not one of the worst I'd seen here, but that wasn't saying much. "We got *cerveza*, we got tequila, all good prices, right? You hand 'em this flyer," he continued, pinning an A5 sheet of paper into my hand, "and your first drink's free! We got titty shows on in there too man, everythin' you wanna see, action round the back if you want it too. You name it, we got it man, what do you like? Boys, girls, young, old? We got 'em from fifteen to eighty in there, right? You ain't never gonna believe your eyes, mano."

I placed a hand on his chest to calm him down some, rested my eyes on his. "What I want," I said calmly, "is a man."

"Shit mano, we got them too, you know? Good prices, men too, no problem , you just –"

"No, *mano*, you got me wrong. I'm looking for one very particular man – Santiago Alvarado. You know him?"

"Yeah mano, I know him," the kid said, the smile gone, "everyone in this fuckin' place knows him, right? But how do *you* know him?"

"We have a . . . *business deal* to discuss," I said with a mischievous smile of my own. "You know? I was told to meet him here."

"Oh," the kid said, the smile returning. "Yeah, Mr. Alvarado, he likes his business."

"Good," I said. "So you can tell me where he is then?"

"Yeah mano, he hangs out in a bar on Cleopatra, place called Casino El Papagayo, it's right on the corner when you come in, just across from the jail. Only it ain't no casino, right?" he said with a wink.

I winked back. "I hear you," I said, and slipped him a hundred pesos for his trouble.

"You sure you don' wanna get a tequila here first, mano?" he said in one last-ditch attempt for custom.

I shook my head. "No, I'm sorry. I'm already late for my meeting with Santiago."

"Okay mano," he said, already turning away from me, flyers extended out toward a pair of locals coming toward him, quickly latching onto the next prospect.

I turned on my heel and started back the way I'd come. The kid had been right, Casino El Papagayo *was* just opposite the guard shack and the jail, I'd seen it when I'd come in. It made sense – direct line of sight to the only entrance to La Zona, and nearby police protection built in.

I picked up the pace as I walked, keen to meet Santiago Alvarado at last.

Chapter Six

Within minutes I had – as planned – got a nice hard bottle of Corona nestled in my right hand. I preferred it to a beer glass – if I had to hit someone with it and it broke, the shape of the bottle was more forgiving than a glass, less likely to put shards into my hands.

The place was just as I imagined it to be – a heaving, neon-lit, beer-stained strip club which seemed to cater almost exclusively for local heavies. There was a long bar against one wall, with plenty of tables and chairs surrounding a wide circular stage in the middle of the large room. Off to the side were private booths, filled with *esses* drinking tequila and smoking joints; on the stage were three naked woman, gyrating around their poles with scant regard for the music. Some men were receiving lap dances at their tables, and money was flying everywhere.

I'd asked at the bar about Santiago, and been pointed in the direction of one of the private booths, over on the far side of the stage. The barman must have radioed across as soon as I'd left, because I was only halfway across the room when two skin-headed, tattooed monsters sidled up next to me, pulling up their baggy shirts to proudly show me their Glock 9mm pistols, settled snuggly into their waistbands.

The presence of Santiago's bodyguards suited me just fine – at least I wouldn't have to look around anymore to find what I was after. They were going to take me straight to him.

"You asking about Mr. Alvarado?" they asked me in Spanish, and I nodded my head.

"Yes," I replied in English. "I'm an American. I have a business proposition for him."

The men looked confused, perhaps unable to understand me; but they cinched in to either side of me and started marching me toward the rear booths, ignoring the girls who danced across the stage just inches away. They'd probably seen such displays so many times now that they were inured to them. Even tits and ass could get boring after a while, I supposed.

They led me toward a private booth, filled with six tough-looking men and three half-naked girls. A fourth girl – fully naked – was giving a lap dance to one of the guys while his buddies cheered. Perhaps some people never got bored of it.

The guy with the girl grinding away on his lap looked across at the two men on either side of me and held up two fingers. *Give me two minutes.* It must have been Santiago, head of this little gang; and as the girl continued to rub herself over him, and his guards continued to jostle me, and his cronies continued to cheer their boss on, I watched him carefully, sizing him up.

He was a good-looking kid, fit and athletic; despite his lifestyle, he obviously kept in decent shape. His eyes were glazed though, as if he'd taken too much of his own shit; and this display in front of his men made me think he was still a kid at heart, and weak with it. I could sense that – despite being in charge here – he really wasn't very far up the ladder. A cartel boss he definitely wasn't, not by a long shot; he was merely a messenger boy for the big shots.

But even messenger boys could be deadly in Nuevo Laredo, and I couldn't be complacent; more people were probably killed in this one nightclub in a single month than in some entire US towns in a year.

I knew the two men either side of me were armed; from the positions of the other men around the booth's table, I couldn't be sure about them. But the table itself was in their way, and would make responding quickly hard to do. Santiago would probably be packing, but I was doubtful of his ability to draw it and bring it into play in the time he would need.

Around the club there was a scattered security presence, but nothing that looked too problematic. The only unforeseen circumstance would be the other patrons, many of whom – despite the police being just across the road – would undoubtedly be armed. But if the shooting started, human nature being what it is would mean that almost everyone would just high-tail it and run. Survival is our most powerful instinct, after all.

I went through my plan of action in my head, centering myself for the task. There were a lot of people, potentially a lot of guns; some of them might know what they were doing, but they wouldn't be *trained*, not in the way I had been. Even now, roaming from town to town, I probably still trained more in one week than those fuckers had in their entire lives.

Wherever I was, I always made sure to stop in at the local martial arts, combat sports and self-defense gyms; boxing, wrestling, Wing Chun, Taekwondo, Karate, Judo, Savate, MMA – you name it, I'd trained in it at some stage over the years. I kept my weapons skills sharp too, visiting any gun range that I could. Some offered long-range targets for the rifle, others were more tactical and combat-oriented, focusing on submachine gun, carbine and pistol work.

I was in great shape, too – my daily curriculum of hiking twenty miles a day was supplemented by a steady diet of hundreds of pushups and sit-ups, with visits to the weights room whenever I got the chance thrown in for good measure.

The people in this room might be carrying the odd pop gun, but when the shit hit the fan, I doubted they would be ready.

I, on the other hand, had *conditioned* myself to be ready; and that was really the only secret to success.

Finally Santiago got bored – or at least more intrigued by what I was there for than he was with the stripper – and sent her on her way with a slap to the ass. She gathered her clothes and pushed past the others, the look on her face suggesting she was glad to be out of there.

Santiago looked across, and my two chaperones gave him a burst of rapid-fire Spanish.

He looked me up and down then, a quizzical look on his eye; he paused to light up a joint, then looked back at me. "You want to discuss business?" he asked in English.

I nodded my head.

"What sort of business a gringo like you want?" he asked, and a couple of his colleagues – presumably the ones who could also speak English – rewarded him with a laugh.

"The business concerning a young girl called Elena Rosales," I replied, eyes never wavering from Santiago's. He met my gaze, eyes still glazed but realization beginning to register. He didn't reply though, just kept looking at me, waiting for more.

I didn't continue though, knowing that if I just kept on staring, he'd break eventually; he was that sort of person.

It took almost a full minute, during which the tension around the table grew with every passing second.

In the end though, Santiago broke just as I knew he would. He waved a hand in the air, the smoke from his joint wafting around the booth, and laughed good-naturedly.

"Yeah, mano, yeah, I think I remember her," he said, concentrating as if he really *was* trying to recall her. "A real sweet piece of ass," he continued with a grin, "I fucked her every way you can imagine, homes, I mean *every* which way, you know? Mmmm," he said, puffing away, "she was a *real* sweet piece of ass."

It was designed to upset me, I knew; and so I just kept on looking at him, my expression set in stone. "Good for you," I said. "So where is she now?"

His eyes narrowed, confused that I wasn't becoming angry. "I don' know, mano," he said evenly, "the little slut's probably bangin' away in some whorehouse right now, I don' know."

"Oh, I think you *do* know."

His glazed eyes flickered, the anger he'd tried to generate in me now reflected across his own features. "Oh yeah?" he shouted. "You think I know? *You* think *I* know? Who you fuck are *you*, eh? Who you to be tellin' me what I fuckin' know and don't know?"

I saw the tilt of the head, knew it was the start of Santiago nodding to the men on either side of me; knew the initial conversation was over. It was Plan B time again.

I *loved* Plan B.

I wrenched my forearm free from the man on my right, smashed him across the face with the bottle; at the same time I pulled free from the man to my left and buried an axe hand right into his throat, the callused edge of my extended hand breaking his trachea.

As the second man fell to the floor, blood gurgling from his throat, I dropped my bottle and reached into his waistband – where he'd been kind enough to show me he was carrying his gun – and pulled the Glock pistol free.

The first guard was recovering from the blow with the bottle, but not for long – I shot him in the chest, dropping him where he stood.

The others around the table were only now starting to react, going for weapons they didn't have a chance of getting into play. The Glock fired once, twice, again and again, the shots deafening in the enclosed space as I took out the men surrounding Santiago; ten shots in five seconds, five more dead men, their bodies slumped over the table, or back against the wall, blood sprayed all over the small booth.

I'd only transitioned to a two-handed grip for the last man, ensuring accuracy for my final shots; he'd had the most time to react, and had almost cleared his own handgun from underneath the table. If he'd shot from underneath the table, he might have had a chance.

Santiago, meanwhile, was rooted to the spot, joint still in his hand, eyes disbelieving. I could hear the chaos behind me as the club started emptying – the girls screaming, the men shouting, everyone running for the exits. Tough, tooled-up *esses*, along with supposedly hardened club security guards, were racing the girls to see who could be first out onto the streets.

I looked back at Santiago, reached forward and

wrenched the table out of the way so that there was nothing left between us. Two bodies rolled down to the floor in a bloody mess, and I stepped over them, the Glock aimed right between the good-looking kid's eyes.

"You going to tell me what you know now, tough guy?" I asked him.

"You don' know what you done, homes," he breathed, obviously scarcely able to believe it himself. "You're dead, don' you know that? *Dead.* You don' know who you fuckin' with, you – "

I cracked him across the face with the pistol, breaking his nose and ruining his pretty features. "Santiago Alvarado, useless little piss-ant dealer for Z201, a crew connected to Los Zetas. You see, Santiago," I said as he whimpered, backing away from me, the joint finally dropping out of his hand, "I *do* know. I just don't give a shit."

I saw him fumbling under his shirt then, obviously – *finally* – going for his own piece. I shot him in the shoulder, the round passing through completely, large clots of blood exploding against the wooden backboard behind him.

Santiago screamed, his gun dropping to the floor; but he was still conscious.

"Tell me where the girl is," I said again, close now, the barrel of my gun pressed against his forehead.

"Please," he gasped, "please . . ."

He grunted in pain, and I pressed the barrel harder into his forehead to remind him that it could still get worse.

"Tell me," I demanded.

"I don' know where she is, man," he managed. "Please . . . I brought her over here one night . . . Last night anyone saw her . . ."

"Where did you take her?" I asked.

"Sanchez . . . he asked for her, I took her to . . . his place . . ."

"Sanchez?" I asked for confirmation. "Who's he?"

"Miguel . . . Ángel Sanchez, he's the . . . head of the *sicarios* for . . . Los Zetas . . ."

It wasn't good news; the sicarios were hitmen, assassins for the cartels. Ruthless and bloodthirsty to the last man. What would they have wanted with the girl?

I could see that Santiago was drifting off into unconsciousness, but I still had to find out more.

"Is Sanchez still here?" I asked him, and was rewarded by a slight nod of his head, but that was all; Santiago was out for the count.

"Drop the weapon!" I heard in angry Spanish from behind me. "Drop it right now!"

I guessed it must be the police; gang members would have just shot me. I let the Glock dangle from a finger and turned to greet them.

It was the cop I'd met at the guardhouse on the way in, along with two of his colleagues; they all had the drop on me, guns leveled at my chest from twenty yards away. To escape, I'd have to regain control of my own weapon and shoot them all before they could react.

I was capable of doing it physically, but morally I'd still not descended that far; shooting cops was still a barrier I was unwilling to cross.

I let the Glock fall to the wooden floorboards with a clatter and raised my hands above my head.

It was time to see what the local jail was like from the inside.

CHAPTER SEVEN

The police station was a relic from ages past, a truly basic place with a single metal desk for paperwork, a big photocopier and fax machine that was about fifteen years out of date, and one large, concrete cell about the right size for five people. Seven were already inside, in varying states of sobriety, and I could see – and then smell – the vomit on the floor.

The prisoners who were still awake eyed me warily, sizing me up. The jail cell was right next door to La Zona's resident sexual health clinic though, so at least I wouldn't have far to go if things *really* went wrong here.

The cops brought me over to the table, where a bespectacled desk sergeant looked up at me with complete disinterest. I may as well have been numbers on the ledger book of an accountant.

"Name?" he asked, and I shrugged my shoulders in

reply.

To his credit, he wasted no more time on the subject; he merely nodded to the three cops who had brought me in, and they rifled my pockets to find some ID.

They pulled out my wallet, fished out a driver's license made out in the name of Thomas B. Meyer, and handed it over to the desk sergeant who started to enter the details. I wasn't unduly worried; by the time they realized that the ID was fake, I hoped to be long gone from here.

The sergeant opened up a fingerprint set next, gestured for me to roll my fingertips over the ink and transfer them to the paper next to it.

This, I thought, was going to be more of a problem, and I hesitated. The cops immediately sprang on me, grabbing my forearm and wrist and forcing my hand toward the ink; I resisted instinctively and received a nightstick in the kidney for my trouble. I relaxed, and a slightly blurred and smudged set of prints were quickly taken.

It might have meant trouble, I knew; a fake ID was one thing, but my fingerprints were quite genuine and would raise alarm bells with the military police, might even be fed back to the FBI. It depended entirely on what they planned on doing with them, and how quickly. It might just have been procedure, prints collected and then forgotten about; or it might be something altogether worse. I really didn't want US law enforcement coming after me here.

Like the other residents of the jail, I had my possessions removed from me, including my belt, socks and shoes; and, processing now over, I was shoved toward the jail cell.

I walked slowly forward, all too aware that as soon as I was in there, I'd be fighting. I picked out the likely candidates, assessed their potential strengths and weaknesses as they looked at me with hungry eyes through the bars.

It was a mistake to be concentrating on what was happening in front of me, what might be happening after I was in there, though; for the real threat was behind me all along.

I sensed the movement behind me, but couldn't avoid it in time; the cop's nightstick caught me heavily around the back of my head, and that was that.

I was out cold.

CHAPTER EIGHT

When I woke up, I was in the slaughterhouse, blindfolded.

And now, after a little beating, I'd had the blindfold ripped off and was looking at a heavily tattooed *esse* clutching a small chainsaw, revving up the rotating blades as his colleagues cheered him on.

You could always rely on the Mexican police, it seemed. I should have killed them when I had the chance.

They must have arrested me simply to keep up appearances; they were always going to hand me over to the cartel. I wondered why they'd fingerprinted me, then realized that it was probably at the request of their paymasters. The cartel bosses would want to know who I was, just in case I didn't talk. The chainsaw, coming closer to my too-weak flesh by the second, was a pretty good interrogation tactic though; the thought of its vicious blades hacking off parts of my anatomy was enough to get me to open up and tell them anything. Hell, I'd describe my first sexual experience for them if they wanted me to.

I don't know why I'd trusted the cops in the first place; I'd already been told that they provided protection for Santiago and his boys. Ah well, I thought sadly; you live and learn.

But if I wanted to live through *this*, I was going to have to act, and act quickly.

I rapidly assessed my situation. My ankles were bound, and my wrists too, behind my back. I was up against a metal wall, but I wasn't secured to anything else, like a chair, and so I was mobile to a certain extent. Now the blindfold was off and my eyes had adjusted to the light, I could also see perfectly.

Things could be worse.

I looked at the gangbangers, taking in the five of them in fractions of a second. One of them was still nursing a sore hand, but he wouldn't let that stop him for long; he was a big, strong guy, like all the others.

They didn't seem to be armed with guns, at least not obviously; and so, if they were, those guns were in pretty inaccessible places and unable to be drawn quickly. But I knew these guys weren't thinking about guns; from the horrific sights of the bloodied and ruined corpses around me, this was obviously a safe haven for them. There were five of them and only one of me, and I was tied up; they wouldn't feel threatened here.

No – this was a place of fists, blunt instruments and blades.

My territory exactly.

I let my eyes go wide in terror – it wasn't hard to do – and began to hyperventilate, laying it on thick. I was dehydrated and it was a struggle, but I managed to force some piss out too, make it look like I'd wet myself through fear, and the guys really loved *that*, pointing and laughing at the gringo who'd pissed himself.

The guy with the chainsaw backed off, and he laughed too; I used the opportunity to talk to him. "Please . . ." I whispered weakly. "Please . . . no . . . I'll talk." I let my voice trail off deliberately, pretending to be on the verge of feinting.

"What?" the guy asked. "What you say?"

"I'll . . . talk," I spluttered, again so quietly that he could barely hear me.

The others kept shouting and jeering, encouraging him to cut an arm off, or a leg, even my dick; but thankfully, the guy with the chainsaw remembered that he actually had a job to do, which meant getting information. He could carve me up at his leisure once I'd given him what he was after.

He let the chainsaw slow down – though didn't turn it off entirely – and grunted at his compadres to keep quiet.

"Say again," he instructed with a jut of his chin, and I repeated the same words, as quietly as I could.

"You better speak up homes, or else I'll take your fuckin' foot clean off," he growled, and I could tell from his eyes that he was serious; he even let the blades come down near to my bound feet. Tied together, if he took one, the other would probably come right off with it; not a pleasant thought.

I'd been trying to sucker him in, to bring his ear close so I could bite down onto it; and if his ear hadn't been close enough, then his nose or his cheek would have done just as well. But – brought up as he undoubtedly had been in a maelstrom of gang violence – he was too street-smart to commit himself fully, and kept his distance.

Clever guy.

But necessity is the mother of invention, and so I did what I always did when my initial plan didn't work – I improvised.

I shifted violently forward on my butt, taking my feet further toward the man, underneath his arms now rather than the chainsaw, and kicked violently upward, my bare feet making contact with those arms, pushing myself off the floor for added leverage.

It worked even better than I'd hoped, the chainsaw looping up back toward the big man and burying itself in his head; his entire body shook with the vibrations as the teeth of the saw rotated viciously into his skull, blood and brains flying everywhere.

I was on my feet in an instant, shoulder barging the dead man backward into his nearest colleague before anyone could react. I dropped to the floor in the stunned silence that followed, kicking the still-live chainsaw across the floor toward the other men. They panicked, skip-stepping out of the way like prima ballerinas, and I used the opportunity to pull my bound arms around my ass, followed by feet and bent knees until I had my hands to my front – far more useful for getting out of this hellhole in one piece.

My ankles were still bound, but I didn't have any time to do anything about that right then; the rest of the gangbangers had finally come to their senses and were flying into action. Two of them came directly for me, while the other two ran for the table of tools; I saw one of them pick up a machete and an icepick, while the other chose a vicious-looking little hatchet.

The first guy was on me and – still prone on the floor – I lashed out with both feet aimed at his leading knee. The blow was hard and I heard the cartilage snap, but he remained standing and so I kicked upward into his balls and he dropped to his knees. I flew at him, burying my teeth into his nose, whipping it from side to side until the tip came off and the man's screams filled the large space, echoing off the metal walls and reverberating round that horrific slaughterhouse like those of the man's own previous victims.

Justice was sweet.

I turned then as the second unarmed man reached me, and spat the tip of his friend's nose into his face; he couldn't help but react, his hands going up to deflect the bloody flesh which flew toward him, his eyes wide in horror. I used the opportunity to make a grab for his leg, pulling it out from under him, and an instant later I was crawling on top of his body, bound hands reaching out for his face, kneeing him in the balls as I went. He convulsed in pain and my hands found his wet, greasy hair a moment later, my fingers entwining within it, using it to control his head as I picked it up and slammed it back into the concrete again and again and again, until blood started to spread out from his skull like a halo.

The other two were almost on me by then, and I knew their blades would be cutting through me in seconds if I didn't move; but my subconscious had already planned my next move for me, and I found myself rolling off the body, scooping up the active chainsaw as I went, controlling it with my two hands, still bound together.

The first man was right there behind me, unable to stop, and I jumped and hopped around – unable to turn effectively with my ankles still tied together – and dropped low at the same time, going to my knees facing the man who was whipping the hatchet through the air toward where my head had just been only moments before.

I used my spin to drive across with the chainsaw, and as it contacted the man's stomach, it went wild in my hands, digging into his flesh and wrestling itself out of my grasp completely; blood spurted into my face and I saw the grey, sausage-like loops of his intestines spilling out of his eviscerated guts onto the hot concrete floor in front of me.

The second armed man was already on me, and I pushed up back to my feet, intercepting his right arm as it descended toward me with the machete; I stopped the blow, but both my hands were tied up while he still had his ice pick free.

In the next instant, the ice pick was whistling in toward my throat, and I did the only thing I could and pulled my arms across to defend the second attack; the machete passed by me, but the ice pick went straight through my right forearm, the pain blinding in its intensity. I saw the tip of the pick emerge on the other side, and I knew it had gone straight through flesh but perhaps missed the bone; and then instinct kicked in and I turned my body in a tight arc, wrenching the handle of the pick out of the man's grip with my movement, continuing the turn as he was still figuring out what I was doing.

And then I was around, full circle, unleashing my bound arms toward him until I buried his own ice pick – still sticking out of my forearm – right into the side of his thick neck, his eyes going wide with shock and pain. He fell to his knees, dragging me painfully down by my forearm with him, and I pulled back with my arms to stop the pain, ripping the pick out of his neck and sending a geyser of arterial blood spraying across the room in front of me.

I looked around to survey the carnage; it wasn't a pretty sight. But then again, the room had been used for this sort of thing before, and the dead men represented just five more bodies for the pitiless slaughterhouse floor.

Better them than me.

I half-waddled, half-hopped, across the floor to the table of torture tools, close to passing out from the pain in my forearm. But I ignored it as best I could and selected a rough saw from the table, gripping it with my teeth and – holding it against the table for resistance – I held up my arms and quickly sawed through the ropes which bound my wrists.

Hands free, I went to work on my ankles and quickly freed my legs. I then stood up straight and walked over to one of the dead gangbangers. I pulled the bandana from his head and put it in my mouth, then pulled the icepick from my arm, biting down on the material to stop me from screaming in pain. From the lack of external intervention during the fight, I assumed we were alone here, but the rag was more for my own pride – I didn't like to hear myself scream any more than I absolutely had to.

The blood ran freely down my arm to my wrist and hand and – trying to ignore the icy pain which seemed to run through my entire body – I secured the bandana around the wound and wrapped it tight in a makeshift bandage.

I looked again at the men to see if any of them were alive to answer questions and saw movement from the man whose nose I'd bitten off, his hands covering his face as he writhed around on the floor. I could hear the high-pitched cries of pain, too.

I approached him, saw it was the guy who'd hurt his knuckles on my teeth. Blood surrounded his face, but his eyes were flickering, his lips moving slightly. A low moan escaped his mouth. He was a mess, but he was alive.

I breathed out slowly, collecting myself.

These people weren't Santiago's, I knew that much – he was a lowdown player, a nobody; this set-up was for professional cartel business.

I needed answers.

And this guy was going to give them to me.

PART THREE

Chapter One

I sipped on an espresso, relaxing into the wicker chair out on the café's outdoor patio as I watched the blood-red sun slowly starting its descent over the horizon.

Half the city was probably looking for me by now, with murder on their mind; but after getting out of that little jam earlier in the day, I felt I'd earned a bit of relaxation time.

I'd bought a med kit from a local pharmacy and fixed my arm up, but it was still painful and I'd struggle to comfortably fire a gun with my right hand for a while. In fact, gripping anything was going to be difficult. Not impossible though, I consoled myself; not impossible.

My ribs were sore from the beating the men had given me, but I didn't think anything was broken. My piss didn't have any blood in it either, so my kidneys must have come through relatively unscathed too.

There was a huge welt on the back of my head from where I'd been knocked out by the cop's nightstick, but it was covered by my hair at least, which was more than could be said for my face. I had nice purple bruises under my eyes, my nose was broken, and one of the guys had knocked a crown out. My jaw and cheekbones had held up okay though.

My nose had been spread halfway across my face, but I'd managed to straighten it back myself, so it now appeared to follow at least some semblance of a straight line. The cartilage was bust up pretty good though, and it made breathing more difficult than it should have been.

The pain itself didn't bother me; it was nothing compared to what had happened years earlier, in another life.

Another world.

My thoughts drifted back there now, the dry heat of the day so similar to Iraq. I tried to fight the memories away, but couldn't; they were too strong.

I'd been in the Rangers for nine years when it happened, the youngest solider to ever make it into the Regimental Recon Detachment – the top unit in an already elite regiment. Not bad for a poor boy from Rock Springs, Wyoming. But then again, maybe my early years in the great outdoors helped – it was a good introduction to working in the field on operations, it put me in tune with nature and exposed me to the necessity of a strong survival mentality from a young age.

That period of my life, while undoubtedly useful,

didn't last long though – my parents were both killed in a car crash before I was seven. I was taken in by my grandparents on my mother's side, and life couldn't have been more different; from a smallholding in Wyoming – poor perhaps, but with the vast plains as my playground – to a rundown apartment in downtown Denver.

Life there was a different kind of hard, and I soon found that surviving in a city was a whole other ball game. My school wasn't great, and there was a lot of pressure to run with the local gangs. I got into some trouble but – to my grandparents' credit – they didn't stand for my behavior at all and went to work overtime on instilling the basic concepts of morality and ethics into my young mind. My grandfather introduced me to boxing too, which was a great way of working off my excess aggression.

I owed them both a lot, and it was a crushing blow when they died. It was my grandfather first, from a heart attack as he was returning from the local grocery store; then my grandmother years later, from cancer. I was halfway around the world on both occasions, fighting al-Qaeda and the Taliban in the deserts, caves and mountains of foreign lands.

I would have liked to be there for them, but it was the life I had chosen. I was sure they would have understood. Indeed, it was my grandfather – himself a veteran of not only World War II but also the Korean War – who had been the one to suggest enlisting in the first place. He could see how the life would suit me, would channel my energies into something useful and positive. I wondered sometimes whether he was right or wrong about that.

I joined the Rangers at the age of seventeen and – unlike most of my intake – I enjoyed the tough, relentless training. Navigation, survival, advanced weapon handling, close combat with knives and bare hands, mountaineering, parachuting, rappelling, fieldcraft and fitness – I loved it all. I passed out as a full-fledged member of the 75th Ranger Regiment not long after my eighteenth birthday and I remember the pride in my grandparents' eyes as they watched the parade, marveling at how their young boy had become a man.

Nearly eight years later, and I had become something else again – a killer.

I was authorized by my government, sure, but that's what I was, and I was damned good at it too. The morality of it never bothered me unduly – I had my orders, and I carried them out. It was always them or me, and I made sure it was never me. It was survival, pure and simple.

Sitting there in the Mexican café, nursing my most recent wounds, my mind took me, unbidden, back to the days following New Year, 2004; when pain became a far bigger part of my life than I had ever imagined possible.

As part of the Regimental Recon Detachment, I'd been situated with my four-man team high up on a hill overlooking a small, walled village a few clicks to the west of Mosul, Iraq's second largest city after Baghdad.

Intelligence assets had hinted that the village was the home of Abdul-Zahir El-Baz, a bomb-maker whose IEDs had taken out more than their fair share of US troops. More than their fair share of civilians too. He was a highly wanted man, and rightly so.

Me and my team had been observing the village day and night for the past three weeks, and we'd come to several conclusions. The first was the fact that El-Baz was indeed located within the village; the second was that his bomb-making factory was also there. Additional to these expected findings though, we had also ascertained that the otherwise unremarkable village was also a major transit point for al-Qaeda troops and some of its low-level leadership.

We'd watched and made our notes, compiling detailed intelligence reports about the target village which we'd been regularly sending back to 3rd Battalion HQ. As lead scout, I'd even been down to the village myself in the dead of night – covered by the team sniper – and placed listening devices within some of the key target houses.

It was these devices which had decided the date of the main Ranger strike mission; for translators had informed our own leaders that a major meeting was scheduled. Plenty of targets would be in the same vicinity, and it would be an opportunity too good to miss.

And so it came to be – at oh-dark-hundred on January 6th 2004, the lightning strike from Delta

Company, 3rd Battalion, 75th Ranger Regiment, began.

It was supposed to be quick, precise, surgical.

Instead, it quickly turned into one big cluster-fuck.

Al-Qaeda were there, ready and waiting for us with the big guns out; Delta Company started to sustain heavy losses almost as soon as their Black Hawks dropped them off inside the village walls. We heard their calls for help over the radio net; heard the gunfire and the screams.

My three colleagues and I had no idea what was going on; how had the enemy known? Our remit was to provide recon, not to get involved ourselves; we were merely observers.

But my friends and I watched the carnage below us, and we all nodded in understanding.

Fuck the rules.

We were going in.

We left Ryan Janes on sniper duties as I raced down the hill with Billy Zito and Tom Cooper to join the combat.

We knew the layout of the streets, the disposition of the buildings, better than we knew our home towns – for more than twenty days, our attention had been rooted on the little walled village.

Through the foggy green haze of our night vision goggles, we tore into the village through a storm drain that ran through an opening in the wall. Our Colt M4A1 carbines up and at the ready, we followed a predetermined route through a maze of alleyways until, at last, we reached the central village square and emerged right into a scene from a horror movie.

There were four wounded soldiers lying in the square – an urban box fifty yards by fifty yards, hemmed in on all sides by rough stone and concrete buildings – and a section of Rangers were sheltering to one side, grabbing whatever cover they could as they got pinned down by enemy fire from the other side. We knew that similar scenes were being played out elsewhere throughout the village, could hear the chatter of AK47s, the controlled bursts of M4s in reply. Mortar fire. Grenades. Rockets. Screams.

Everything had gone to hell in a handbasket, and all we could do was wade in and hope for the best. There was sniper fire coming from a tall building to the right, and I called in the details to Janes who – from faraway on the hill – immediately started taking shots at the suspected window. Under the conditions, it was unlikely he would hit anything, but it quietened things down for the few moments we needed.

I got on the comms link to Delta Company, gave them the brief on what we were doing; then, just to be sure, I shouted instructions to the section of men holed up in the far corner.

"Cover us!" I yelled, and – despite their own predicament – I was pleased to see they responded immediately and opened up with all guns blazing.

Under the hail of gunfire, the three of us raced out from the alleyway, getting to the center of the square in world championship time. Zito and Cooper got their free hands on one soldier each, still firing back single-handed with their M4s.

As they dragged the men back across the open ground, rounds from the enemy landing all around them despite the best efforts of the Delta section, I slung my own rifle behind me and grabbed both remaining men, a hand on each of their collars.

I dragged them backwards, blood smearing over the ground, appearing as a black sludge through the goggles. I heard a cry to my left, saw that Zito had been hit, right through the chest; he was on the floor next to the soldier he'd been hauling, gasping for breath. I couldn't be sure if he'd taken it in the vest, had no idea if he would live; but I was relieved to see other men leaving the safety of cover, grabbing Zito and the other guy and pulling them back to safety.

Cooper got there next, handing over the man and getting right back on his rifle, covering me as I too made it to safety – although I soon learned that it was a relative term. The area of cover was nothing more than a recess between buildings, just a couple of dozen square feet of space with no way out. To escape would mean crossing the open ground of the square; but to remain ran the risk of a direct attack by the enemy onto our position. Just one rocket-propelled grenade sent our way would finish us off without much difficulty.

"How is he?" I shouted to Cooper, who was bent over Zito.

Cooper shook his head, and I could see that the heavy breathing of Zito was over, the chest still. "Dead," Cooper said, with as much control as he could muster. "Round got him in the fuckin' throat."

Shit. I'd been wrong about the chest after all; he'd been shot in the damn neck.

I quickly went through my options; more than quickly, actually – it was that subconscious thing again, running unbidden through so many options that the conscious brain would never have managed to cope.

And then I was moving.

Through the confusion and the chaos, I had seen that most of the shots had been coming from a tall building to the left of center, a few over from the location of the sniper.

As I raced away from safety – unbidden, unplanned, my mind doing its own thing, forcing my body to follow it – I was stunned by a blast to my right, a huge concussive explosion that rocked me to my bones.

"Shit yeah," came Janes' voice over my comms system. "I wasn't getting anywhere with my little rifle, so I used the AT4. Son of a *bitch.*"

Good old Janes – too far for his night vision to give him a proper target for his sniper rifle, he'd simply taken our section's M136 AT4 light anti-tank weapon and let rip with its 84mm high explosive anti-armor warhead. *Son of a bitch* was right – that sniper wasn't getting any more shots off. As I looked across, I saw the façade of the building cratered, concrete blasted, windows shattered.

"Thanks," I barked back, legs still pumping as I raced across the square, grateful for suppressive fire from the boys behind me as I went.

I was reaching the building I wanted, close now, so close; rounds were flying around me, but so far – somehow – I still hadn't been hit.

And then I was there, and it was only then that I realized Cooper was right by my side, having made the suicide run just behind me.

I saw him smile through my night vision goggles. "You didn't think I'd let you have all the fun, did you?" he asked.

I smiled back, nodded my head in appreciation.

It was then that Cooper's face exploded across my own; I literally saw the eyeballs leave their sockets, the cheek bones shattering outwards as a blast of blood flew out of my friend's shattered features, covering me in gore; and then I felt the pain, knew the bullet had passed through Cooper's skull, exited his face and nicked me on the side of the neck on the way through.

There was another explosion, and another section of the right-hand building was cratered by the AT4. "Fuck," came Janes' voice, "fuck, I'm sorry man, sniper must have moved in time, missed with the first one. *Fuck.*"

My hand went to my neck, came away black with blood in the green haze of the goggles; but I was still standing, which was more than could be said for Cooper. But I couldn't think about him now, couldn't afford to waste the time, couldn't let myself break mentally, lose the momentum, lose the aggression.

"I'm going in," I said, and that was it; I turned,

braced myself and – *boom* – the door was open, my boot smashing straight through it.

What happened next was almost a mystery to me, my body taking over completely, mind on autopilot, responses and reflexes operating on a purely instinctive level.

I saw two men racing down the stairwell toward me, and then they were gone, blasted back by my M4; and then I was past them, taking the stairs three at a time. Four more men on the next landing, firing AKs toward me, lethal 7.62mm rounds buzzing around me but never touching; my own trigger finger sure, aim steady, men dropping before me like ten pins, black blood spilled over the walls in buckets.

I cleared the rooms, checking, shooting, checking, shooting, changing magazines in the blink of an eye and then shooting again, body after body hitting the floor in my wake.

Room after room, floor after floor, my rifle an extension of me, so many men before me, muzzle blasts exploding violently across the goggles, flashes of light followed by more dead bodies.

The rifle dropped from my hands, and I barely realized why; but my left arm no longer responded and I instantly drew my Sig Sauer pistol and carried on fighting.

I continued to move upstairs, now on the fourth and final floor; and as soon as I got there I felt a white hot pain in my guts, felt my pistol fire in my good hand, felt another pain in my shoulder, fired again, saw men go down; saw three more with rifles, saw my handgun erupt at them, saw them hit the floor; watched in disbelief as one pulled himself up and came at me with a blade, running toward me, my own body sluggish now, moving slower; and then I coughed and jerked as the blade entered my bowels, jerked inside me, tore upwards; without knowing what I was doing, I clamped hold of my enemy in a death grip, felt the icy pain deep inside me, and ran with him toward the window, felt the glass smash as we crashed through it, felt the air whistling past us as we plunged toward the hard ground below.

We hit moments later, the man with the knife first, his body only slightly cushioning the impact.

But that was it; my battle was over.

And it would be two weeks before I eventually woke up again.

CHAPTER TWO

When I finally came out of my coma, I began to wish I hadn't.

Cooper was dead, and so was Zito; the Rangers finally won the battle, but the losses were great. Twelve men killed in all, a terrible tragedy. A terrible night. And to top it all off, the promised al-Qaeda leadership hadn't even been there.

It had all been for nothing.

Fifty-six of the enemy had been killed though, so I supposed it wasn't a total loss. It transpired that my own actions had accounted for roughly half that amount; when the village had been secured and daylight came, the building I'd raided had been a charnel house, corpse piled on bloody corpse.

My own body was wrecked as a result though – one 7.62 round through the left bicep, another through the shoulder, another tearing through my stomach and coming out through a kidney. The knife had done plenty of damage too, and I was horrified to be pissing and shitting into a bag, my own bowels unable to process anything.

My skin had been cut to ribbons by the broken window glass, and the four-story fall to the square below had broken most of the major bones in my body.

It was a miracle, the doctors all said unanimously, that I had survived at all.

But at least my efforts hadn't been in vain; with the main enemy force taken out, the Ranger section went back into action and re-took all the other buildings in the square, before moving out toward other sectors to assist other teams. The citation for the Congressional Medal of Honor that they gave me for what I did that day cited my "courage in the face of enemy fire", my "inspirational leadership", my "incredible combat performance", and credited my actions as having reunited the effort of US forces to win the battle.

Despite the congratulations, the adulation, the respect, the glory, my mind didn't fare much better than my body though – I'd lost my friends, lost parts of myself. How do you handle that?

I was in hospital for months, had to learn to walk again, to eat again, to use the toilet again; but eventually I did recover, and I did leave.

The mental scars were harder to get rid of though, and I didn't know how to handle it – they offered me counselling but, like many soldiers, I declined the help.

And when it was forced upon me, I just went through the motions, unable to help myself. I didn't feel I deserved it; I should have died with my friends.

We'd provided the intelligence after all, we'd been the ones to tell HQ about the place, to suggest the raid. It was our fault.

Even when it later turned out that the man who'd been translating the transcripts from my listening devices for the battalion commander had actually been playing both sides of the fence, had actually been an al-Qaeda agent feeding information back about our recon efforts to his terrorist friends, the knowledge didn't help. The traitorous Iraqi translator had been arrested and thrown into Guantanamo Bay – and had later turned up dead, allegedly beaten by other inmates but more likely than not tortured to death – but it still didn't help me sleep any better.

I was upset about Bobby Zito, and even more so about Tom Collins; he had been my best friend, I'd been best man at his wedding, was the godfather to his three kids. I'd promised him that I'd look after his family if anything happened to him, but what good was I now? My military career was over, and what else could I do?

I left the service finally in 2005 with a hearty slap on the back and one hundred grand in my back pocket – twenty months of severance pay for ten years of duty. I gave it all to Tom's wife and kids; they needed it more than I did.

My body was healing, but it was difficult to find

work; nobody in the real world cared if you had the Medal of Honor, or if you had two clusters to your Purple Heart; they didn't care of you could hit a bullseye at six hundred yards with a hundred different weapons, or if you could survive in the wild as long as you had to. What use was the ability to drink sap from tree bark, or to know how to kill a man silently with a knife, to a factory owner, or an office manager?

And so I'd gone from place to place, and from one lowly-paid job to another. Day laborer, bouncer, dock hand, delivery driver, grill chef – I did it all. But nowhere wanted me permanently, nobody was willing to take me on and give me a proper contract, proper terms of employment.

But then – eventually – I got a job in a meat-packing factory; regular work at last, and I began to settle down, rented out a little trailer and – with some unlicensed pit-fights down at the slaughter yard on the side – started saving a bit of money.

I took another sip of my espresso, which was cold now, and considered carrying on with that line of thought; but, knowing where it was going, I finally snapped out of it and brought myself back to the here and now, on the café patio.

But I knew pain, and pain knew me; it was safe to say that, at least. A couple of black eyes and a broken nose were nothing, in the overall scheme of things; it was all about keeping things in proportion.

Everything was relative, and what I'd experienced in the past day or so wasn't really up there with the

worst things to have happened to me.
Not by a long shot.

CHAPTER THREE

I wore sunglasses to cover the bruises under my eyes, as well as to help disguise my features from the casual observer, and I wore a peaked baseball cap. I'd also bleached my hair and applied a copious amount of fake tan to my usually pale skin, so that I looked very little like the man who had entered Nuevo Laredo the previous day.

I had to assume that the police were looking for me, as well as the cartel's hitmen and petty gangsters. Such a simple disguise wouldn't throw them off the scent forever, but it was better than nothing. And what were they going to do? Stop and interrogate every foreigner in the city?

It was actually possible, and I'd already decided to abandon my hotel room; the police might well be going door to door asking questions, and I didn't want to get caught out again. It was a shame that I'd lose my things, but I'd stocked up on weapons back in the slaughterhouse; that table was like an Aladdin's Cave of violent goodies.

I wasn't really relaxing as I sat outside the café, actually; I was still working, waiting for Miguel Ángel Sanchez to show himself. He was eating an early dinner at Koto Sushi, across the wide and busy Avenida Reforma from my little café.

When my friend with the damaged hand and nose had talked, back in the slaughterhouse just a few short hours before, it was the second time I'd heard the name Miguel Ángel Sanchez.

It made sense; Santiago must have alerted him, or told the police, and they'd passed me onto his cronies. And from what I'd recently heard, it wasn't a smart move to get on his shit list.

Whereas Z201 were just regular street hoods, the parent organization of Los Zetas – for whom Sanchez did his work – was the real deal.

Its genesis could be found in the late 1990s when a group of elite Mexican Army commandos deserted and joined the Gulf Cartel as armed enforcers, before forming their own criminal organization in 2010. Unlike most gangs, they brought military organization, training and tactics into the criminal underworld, and took power through ruthless and systematic armed warfare.

Only half of their wealth was generated by the drug business, as they had their fingers in every pie imaginable – from pirated DVDs to human trafficking, and from local shakedowns to organized kidnappings, Los Zetas did it all.

To help enforce their domination, the cartel – presumably due to its military background – even ran training camps for its hitmen, who were known as *sicarios*. They were taught how to kill with a knife, a garrote, and with a wide variety of guns. A favored tactic was shooting from a fast-moving motorcycle – all the better to sweep through traffic and avoid police pursuit – and such skills were also practiced widely at the camps.

Miguel Ángel Sanchez had been Los Zetas' number one hitman in his day, with a total body count numbering in the hundreds, including several more complex kills including political, law enforcement and military officials. He'd plied his trade for years, and had got away with it every time.

He was now semi-retired from active duty, and instead helped train and organize a new generation of sicarios, which gave him the same status as one of the second-tier bosses within the cartel, a position of great power.

I would have to tread carefully; he wasn't just connected, he was actually dangerous too. Like the original army deserters, Sanchez had been a member of the elite *Grupo Aeromóvil de Fuerzas Especiales*, the Special Forces Airmobile Group. He was well-trained and – perhaps more importantly – vastly experienced.

I wondered, again, what he'd wanted with Elena Rosales. Had he seen her one night, demanded that she be brought to him for his own pleasure? Or had he brought her as a special treat for his men? She'd been just thirteen at the time, and the thought made me want to kill them all.

I also wondered where she was now, what had happened to her over the past three years. Was I wasting my time here? Would I ever get the answers I wanted? That her family *needed*?

But I cut out the doubts as soon as they reared their ugly little heads. I'd taken the money, and I had a job to do. I would find Elena, or at least find out what had happened to her, and nothing in this world was going to stop me.

Not even Miguel Ángel Sanchez and his dreaded sicarios.

Chapter Four

I was halfway through my third espresso when Sanchez emerged from Koto Sushi, red-faced and angry. He was shouting into his cellphone, then shouting at two of the six men he'd left the restaurant with, then shouting back into his cellphone. I couldn't hear what was being said from across the road, but the man definitely wasn't happy

I put down my demitasse with a slight smile, hoping that I was the reason for the man's displeasure.

It stood to reason – it would be about now that the reports would be coming back from the slaughterhouse. Five of his own men dead – for despite the fact that the guy without the nose had supplied me with information, I'd decided the world was better off without him and sent him to visit his four buddies in the hereafter – and the supposed victim was up and gone, nowhere to be found.

Sanchez was heavier than I'd imagined, a short pot-bellied man whose youthful muscle had turned to fat; and yet he still moved with a fluid grace that indicated his years of training, the command he still possessed over his own body. He'd let himself go a bit perhaps, but he still looked lethal.

He wore a lightweight cotton suit, expensive blue shirt open at the chest, gold flashing underneath from more than one chain. His fingers were the same, adorned in gold rings; and I assumed that he wore them more for the knuckle-duster effect than as a fashion statement. Everything was practical with men like that.

His long hair was slicked back, and his swarthy features were dark, brooding and brutal; he was not a handsome man by any token, but he displayed a kind of animal magnetism that defied his physical appearance. I knew what it was; it was the unbreakable, unshakeable and impossible-to-fake confidence that came from having killed people with his own two hands, in sufficient numbers for him to have a heightened sense of immortality, of his superiority over other men.

I made a mental note again of how dangerous the man might be, then stood up, peeled off some bills to pay for my drinks and left them on the table behind me.

Sanchez and his men were heading for the cars parked around the outside of Koto Sushi, two Cadillac sedans and a black Mercedes. I wasn't surprised to see the door of the Mercedes opened for Sanchez, who slid into the back seat as his driver and bodyguard went upfront.

Two more men went in each Cadillac, and the convoy pulled out onto Avenida Reforma, Sanchez in the middle car, protection at the front and rear. Good tactics.

I was already in my own vehicle, an old Honda SUV I'd stolen from a long-term parking lot, and I pulled out into traffic after the convoy, careful to leave a couple of cars in between me and my target. If I followed too closely, they would spot me easily; the trick was always to hold back. They might still see me, but that was a risk I had to take; following a target by yourself was hard and risky work, much harder than when you did it with a team. Then again, you had to play with the cards you'd been dealt, and I was on my own.

I didn't know whether Sanchez would want to go and investigate the scene at the slaughterhouse himself, or whether he'd go and see his bosses; whether he'd visit one of the bars or nightclubs he ran, or whether he'd just go home. But no matter; I'd follow patiently and wait for my opportunity.

It soon became apparent that he *was* on his way to the slaughterhouse, as we seemed to be travelling the reverse of the route I'd used when I'd escaped. The little torture chamber was situated in an old cattle slaughterhouse, part of an abandoned farm in the countryside outside Nuevo Laredo, just south of Quetzalcoatl International Airport.

When I'd escaped, I'd taken one of the cars I'd

found in the courtyard outside, keys still in the ignition and obviously belonging to one of the men I'd just killed. I'd driven that car back into the city, left it in a side street – unlocked and with the key still in the ignition as I'd found it – then located and stolen the Honda.

We were headed for the airport now, travelling south along Route 85 before going west on Boulevard Aeropuerto. The traffic was busy here, and I had no trouble flitting in and out from a distance, keeping the convoy in my sights ahead of me; three big vehicles in a row might be good for protection, but they were easy to follow. But with the amount of vehicles on the road, and with the daylight fading fast, I knew I would be harder to spot.

If I carried on along the dusty countryside roads after the convoy though, I would immediately begin to stand out; and so as we drew nearer, I refreshed my memory of the area and chose my plan accordingly.

Sure enough, the convoy pulled off the main road before reaching the airport. I was still okay to follow for a while – the sun was almost gone now, headlights were on, and identification would be more difficult for the guys up front – but soon, I would have to change tactics. After all, I didn't want to catch up to them and take them all on. They would all be armed with handguns at a minimum, and probably had much more in their cars – machine pistols, assault rifles, shotguns. All I had were the semi-medieval bladed weapons I'd taken from the slaughterhouse, along with a single handgun that I'd found in the waistband of one of the men I'd killed.

The FN Five-SeveN was an effective weapon, and a favorite of the cartels due to its alleged ability to penetrate the body armor of law enforcement and military personnel. It was disputed whether that was indeed true, but it gave the pistol a reputation that the gangs wanted to have a piece of; its "cop killer" moniker suited them perfectly. Its lethality was not due to having a large caliber, but the reverse. At only 5.7mm – hence the pistol's designation – the round travelled at enormous speed, which contributed to its penetrating power. At muzzle velocities of over two thousand feet per second, the effect of the little bullet could be devastating. The size of the long, narrow rounds also had an additional benefit – a magazine capacity of twenty rounds, much more than conventional pistols.

It was less than I would need against seven men though, and so – for the moment at least – I decided that discretion was the better part of valor, and I would keep my distance. The abandoned farm was up a small dirt road that didn't carry on any further; if Sanchez and his men wanted to leave at any point, they would have to come back the same way they'd come.

I therefore decided to pull over on the last metaled road, and watched the convoy roll off into the distance. I doused my headlights and sat tight, aiming to follow them when they returned. Maybe they'd lead me back to Sanchez's home, or else another cartel hideout; any intelligence I could gather would be good.

But then, as I sat there in my car, I began to see things differently. I was on the clock now – my fingerprints had been taken, and I had no idea who they'd been fired off to. The FBI might be on their way here right now.

There was also the fact that the cartels were also after me already, and the longer I spent south of the border, the more likely it was that I'd end up as yet another one of the headless corpses that the gangs left in their wake. And I would be damned if I was going to let that happen.

I reassessed the situation in light of this. As it stood, my target – Miguel Ángel Sanchez – was right now in an abandoned farm at the end of a dead-end dirt track. There were six men with him, but there was no other way out for them, no ingress or egress except that single narrow road. If I could take him there, I would have the luxury of being able to interrogate him in a relatively safe environment. If I followed him home, who knew how well protected he'd be?

I reassessed my weapon again too – it had twenty rounds, and there *were* only six people that I needed to put out of commission. It wasn't beyond the realms of possibility.

But then I remembered that Sanchez must have got the word about what I'd done from someone, and that someone might well still be there too. And how many *someones* might there be? The trouble was, I had no way of knowing. I didn't want to turn up and be faced with an entire platoon of gun-toting sicarios.

On the other hand, I was running out of time and – despite my years of subtle recon work – times had changed, and I was no longer the patient man I once was.

I looked down at the FN pistol that had appeared, unbidden, in my hand, felt the knives and blades that were secured to my body, and came to a decision.

I was going in.

CHAPTER FIVE

The sun was gone now, and the land was dark once again; perfect for a man like me, and for what I had to do.

I'd left the SUV parked at the end of the dirt lane, blocking off access to the farm. It wouldn't stop people forever, but it would certainly delay Sanchez and his men leaving, or others arriving.

I moved swiftly across the open fields and dirty scrubland, keeping low at all times, careful never to silhouette myself. I knew where the light came from – where the moon was, where the clouds were, from which direction shone the lights of Nuevo Laredo's urban sprawl – and I used it to my advantage, coming across the countryside at just the right angles to be invisible, a silent and unseen wraith coming to wreak havoc and mayhem on the enemy.

I hoped.

If Sanchez and his men were using night vision goggles, I might not be quite as invisible as I'd hoped. But there was no real reason to suspect that this was the case; Sanchez had left dinner after the call and hadn't stopped to pick up any equipment, and I knew that the slaughterhouse didn't have such sophisticated items.

Besides which, I could see electric lights up ahead, and I knew that the slaughterhouse lights would be on full, car headlights also aimed around the rest of the farm. People like that didn't like darkness any more than the next person; and Sanchez would want to have a good look at what I'd done.

I considered that he might send out patrols to look for me, but with limited men – and at night – I didn't think he'd make that call. He was an expert in death too, and would probably be able to tell that his men had been killed many hours before, that whoever had done it would be long gone by now.

He had no reason to suspect that I was coming back.

Besides which, even if there were patrols, I was confident that I would hear them before they could see me. Range with night vision goggles wasn't great, while sound travelled a long way at night, across open terrain. And my own eyes were adjusted to the dark now, enabling me to move swiftly and surely across the arid land.

I could hear the sounds coming from the farm already, Sanchez's voice loud and demanding, the voices of his cohorts explanatory, pleading.

Sanchez was pissed – five of his men had been killed, and he would have no idea who'd done it, or why; and a man like that *hated* not knowing.

I was getting close now, picking through thorny bushes and gliding across red-topped soil, the illuminated buildings already in my sights.

I slowed myself, edging forward more cautiously, all too aware that Sanchez might have sentries posted, that the light from the car headlamps was spilling out into the land around the farm, creating a network of light and shadow. I had to be sure that I monitored it carefully; the last thing I wanted was to be caught at the wrong point, for my body to be illuminated or for my shadow to suddenly appear in front of Sanchez and his men.

I came closer and closer, crawling now, low beneath the high, burnt grasses that bordered the farm, moving so slowly that my progress was barely noticeable. I could hear the voices more loudly now, and translated the Spanish immediately in my head.

"He's not going to fucking be here, you idiots!" Sanchez shouted. "Those men were killed this morning! He'll be halfway to fucking Acapulco by now!"

"What do we do?" came another voice.

"Now?" Sanchez replied. "Now? Now we *think*. The police should get the ID from those prints soon, then we'll know who this fucking guy is, then we might start to understand what the fuck is going on."

I was at the border now, the decrepit, broken-down

fence that ran around the main yard, and I could see clearly into the brightly lit central courtyard where the cars had parked up.

There was the Mercedes, the two Cadillacs, and another car which I recognized as belonging to the men I'd killed. In addition, there were two other vehicles, a big Ford pickup and a Toyota sedan. Presumably, they belonged to the men who'd discovered the bodies and notified Sanchez.

The pickup only had a front cabin, so would have had two occupants maximum. Worst case scenario for the sedan was five, two up front and three in the back. So there were possibly seven more men in there, in addition to Sanchez and the other six. Which gave me fourteen possible enemy combatants; not favorable odds by any stretch of the imagination.

Twenty rounds, I told myself. *You've got twenty rounds in the FN.*

You could shoot them all and still have six left over.

I almost laughed at that. I was good, but not that good.

Especially as I saw the sort of hardware the men were carrying, tooled up with another cartel favorite, the AR15 assault rifle. Thirty round mags of .223 Remington that could be emptied on full-auto in just three seconds; dangerous little toys, and they all seemed to be carrying them.

I could see Sanchez holding court, unarmed, in the center. Around him stood two of the six men he'd come with, and three others I didn't recognize. I couldn't see anyone else, but could hear voices echoing from the barns and outbuildings that dotted the area, and knew they must be doing a search of the farm, just in case I was holed up there. It was possible; I might have been injured, and unable to escape any further. The men who'd arrived on the scene first were probably showing the new arrivals around, pointing out how careful they'd been in their own initial search.

Which meant that men were spread out around the area. Armed, yes; but probably unprepared.

I could narrow down the odds here, I thought happily, and put the FN pistol back into my waistband, stalking around the fence line, the sounds of shouted Spanish from the courtyard covering my movement.

It was time to start executing my plan.

[]

CHAPTER SIX

I took the first man quickly, stalking him from behind, matching my movement to his until I was just inches away; and then my hand went around the man's mouth as the ice pick went up into the base of his skull at the first cervical vertebra, severing the spine and his entire nervous system with one firm thrust.

I felt the body spasm and relax, and bent at my knees, lowering the already dead man silently to the floor.

We were in a large barn, unused for years, full of junk, old farm vehicles and scrap metal. The men were using flashlights, and I scooped the dead man's out of his hands and pressed onward.

The second man was just a few feet away, completely unaware of what had just happened to his colleague. I walked toward him, flashlight shining directly into his face, making it impossible for him to see who was behind it.

"Take that fucking light out of my eyes, esse!" the man said, arm reflexively covering his face; but I carried on forward, flashlight up until the moment I reached him, at which point I dropped the light and stabbed the ice pick through his eyeball and straight into the brain.

Again, the man dropped dead instantly. I took the man's AR15, so like the M4 that had become almost a part of me over the years, and slung it over my shoulder. I would use it, but not yet; I was in silent mode at the moment, and an assault rifle was seldom quiet.

I went to the first man, took the magazine from his weapon and pocketed it. They didn't have any more ammo on them, but I was happy with what I had; it was substantially more than I'd had a few moments before.

I turned my flashlight off and slipped out of the barn's broken woodwork into the night beyond, moving toward sound to my right.

I saw a brick outbuilding and headed over that way, noting through the half-broken windows how light bounced around inside. The door was open, and I maneuvered myself close, sure to time it right, enter the building when the light was aimed away from the entrance.

I chose my moment well, inside before the lone man knew I was there; and I once more matched my movement to his, pacing up behind him, my hand again going up to secure the mouth while my ice pick did the rest of the work, although this time – due to having less light, and therefore somewhat diminished accuracy – my target was not the brain stem but the kidney.

The result was equally effective, the man's body convulsing with the sudden shock and white hot pain before relaxing into oblivion.

I took the magazine out of his weapon too. Waste not, want not.

I moved quickly out of the building, watched from the shadows as Sanchez and his two men moved toward the slaughterhouse – perhaps to have one final look before they moved out.

That left three remaining by the cars; with three dead, and the group that had just left, there were possibly five more unaccounted for.

I was just working through my next set of actions when I sensed movement to my right, moved just instants before the flashlight beam would have lit me up like Christmas. But I couldn't take the risk of it happening again and so – with the beam leading me – I pulled out a long, serrated knife and launched myself forward.

I trapped down the flashlight hand, using the sensation of the touch as a range-finder before I unleashed the knife, whipping it across in front of me to the point where I knew the man's throat would be.

I was dead-on – there was a slight gargle, and I felt warm, sticky blood splatter across my face. The man dropped to his knees, then rolled onto his side, dead.

That had been lucky; I hadn't heard the man coming, and if his flashlight had been a few inches over, he might well have shot me before I would have had time to react.

I was going to have to be even more careful if I wanted to come out of this thing alive.

Keeping out of the way of the three men in the courtyard, I worked my way over to the slaughterhouse, peered in through a grimy window.

The lights were on, and it looked just the same as when I'd left it; no effort had been made to move the fresh bodies. And why would Sanchez bother? The men had failed him and – in his eyes at least – he owed them nothing, not even the courtesy of a decent burial.

I saw the other four men in there too, and felt relieved – everyone had now been located. Three outside in the courtyard, Sanchez and six others in the slaughterhouse.

I quickly weighed things up, deciding which group to take out first.

And then, my mind made up, I moved.

Chapter Seven

I used the flashlight trick again, shining it toward the men by the car and hoping that – holding the AR15 – my silhouette would be indistinguishable from one of the cartel members.

I walked forward with confidence, copying the cocky gait of the men I'd observed, carrying myself as if I had all the right in the world to be there.

The men weren't positioned perfectly, but it could have been worse. One stood at the side of the Ford pickup, while the other two were at the front, leaning against the hood.

The one by the side told me to turn off the fucking flashlight, followed by arm-waving and muttered complains from the two by the hood, but by then I was just a few feet away.

It was a risky strategy that I was engaged in, and I

would have to move fast, just about as fast as I was capable of moving – but if it paid off, it would be worth it.

Just one foot away from the first man now, and I could see his suspicions were starting to be aroused, but it was too late. I dropped the flashlight on the floor and – human nature being what it is – he couldn't help but watch as it fell.

In that momentary distraction, I plunged the knife deep inside his chest, tip piercing his heart and killing him before it could beat again.

My other blade, a Bowie-style knife, was already arcing its way through the air as the men leaning on the hood eventually reacted, and it sliced straight through the first man's neck and dropped him to the floor even as it reversed its momentum and cut back toward the second man.

But he was faster than his friend and managed to get his rifle up to block the blow. Fearful that if he got a shot off and alerted everyone then all hell would break loose, my free hand immediately came down, impacting hard onto the rifle and making him drop it to the dusty ground.

I spiked in again with the knife but the man was quick and dodged the blow, reaching out to grab my wrist with a powerful, meaty hand that threatened to break my arm in two.

In the crisscross light of the gathered headlamps, I saw that the man was about to shout out to warn his friends and I launched my head forward, butting him straight in the face to keep him quiet, his words melting away into a tiny whimper of pain.

But still he held my arm, and he punched me hard in the gut with his other hand. He drew it back to punch me again when I remembered that I had a spare hand too – and in the space he'd provided with his pull-back, I shot the bunched fingertips of that hand up into the nerve cluster between his neck and his jaw.

He didn't let go of my knife arm, but he did stagger back – which gave me just enough room to reach into my waistband and pull out yet another weapon from the medieval arsenal I'd taken from the slaughterhouse.

The small meat cleaver parted the air with a low whistle, then parted the man's skull with a solid *clunk*, blood, brain and fragments of bone flying across the pickup's hood as the man's eyes went wide in disbelief.

They were still open when his dead body hit the floor, head split open like a watermelon.

Pretty? No.

Effective? Absolutely.

I paused to gather myself, quiet, senses tuned in. Had anyone heard me? Was anyone coming to investigate?

But there was nothing, just three dead bodies scattered around the pickup. I rolled them underneath, out of the light of the headlamps, just in case anyone looked out of the slaughterhouse windows, or came outside for a smoke.

I breathed out slowly, steadily, as I took in the final target.

The slaughterhouse. Present home to Miguel Ángel Sanchez and six of his goons.

I pocketed the blades, checked my FN pistol was sitting snuggly in my waistband, and made ready with the AR15.

This was it.

Time to party.

CHAPTER EIGHT

I rested by the main double doors, rusty metal things that looked like they'd fall off at any moment; there was no reason for stealth now, things had gone beyond that.

By going through the front, I would at the same time be closing off the main avenue of escape for the cartel men inside. By then, I no longer had any doubt in my mind about succeeding in what I had to do; there was no room for doubt, no room for backing out now. I was committed, and with that commitment came a change in mindset. Nothing was going to stop me; it might be seven to one, but I wouldn't be escaping from them, they would be trying to escape from me.

Aggression. Aggression. *Aggression.*

I took a deep breath, visualized the positions of the men in the room in my mind's eye, and spun around quickly, kicking open the old iron doors.

My sudden entry caught the men off guard, and I immediately shot the first two in the chest before they'd moved an inch, tracking the AR15 across to the next man and catching him in the face and neck.

The other three were moving now, trying to find cover, to mobilize their own weapons; but I still had the advantage of momentum and pressed on, switching to burst fire on the rifle, keeping heads pinned down while I identified viable targets.

Sanchez – despite his lack of condition – had been the first to move, a pearl-handled Colt .45 appearing in his hands as he rolled across the floor to the table of torture tools, upending it and using it as cover. A smart move.

Another man wasn't so quick to respond though, and I nailed him through the heart with a burst of controlled fire.

I felt the hot air of a .45 round sail past my face and knew Sanchez was entering the fight; I responded with a burst of .223 into the table, then turned to see another man fleeing through the main doors while the remaining thug drew a bead on me with his own rifle.

I shot toward him, aiming for center mass and instead hitting the rifle itself, spinning it out of his hands. I knew that I'd used the last rounds from that magazine, that I would have to reload; but the last man was already running toward me, just feet away, a stiletto dagger having appeared in his hands almost as if by magic.

As he reached me and swiped the dagger toward

my throat, I responded by turning the rifle into a blunt trauma weapon, smashing it butt-first into his oncoming face, its range longer than the stiletto's.

As the man staggered back, his face bleeding, his nose shattered, I heard the roar of a car engine, the movement of headlamps out in the courtyard; saw a blur of movement as Sanchez raced for the double doors, firing blind as he went. The rounds went nowhere near me, but I knew he'd only intended them to cover his exit; for all he knew, there was a whole bunch of us coming to get him, and his natural instinct was to flee. The first man who'd run had just been getting the car ready for his boss, and now they were both about to hightail it out of there.

The SUV I'd left at the bottom of the lane would only stall them for so long; I had to finish this and get off after them as quickly as possible.

The man in front of me stopped moving backward and, hand still on the dagger, came charging at me again; but I'd already been moving, ejecting the empty mag from the AR15 and retrieving another from my pocket; he was almost on me as I slipped the fresh mag in, let the working parts go forward, and pressed the trigger.

The rounds hit the man from nearly point-blank range, the dagger just inches from my face, and dropped him on the spot, guts torn from his belly, steam rising from his internal organs as he hit the floor.

Wasting no time surveying my handiwork, I turned on my heel and ran out into the warm night, watching the tail lights of one of the Cadillacs as it tore out of the courtyard toward the dirt track that would take them to the main road beyond.

I knew that, if they rammed it hard enough, they might just be able to blast the SUV out of the way and carry right on; and so I let rip with a burst of .223, shooting out the rear windows and at least one of the rear tires. The vehicle slewed first to one side, then to the other, but carried on going, and I turned to the Mercedes and wrenched open the driver's side door, glad to see the keys still in the ignition. I knew why the men left their keys there – who would steal a car from a member of the cartels?

I threw the assault rifle onto the passenger seat, turned the key and gunned the engine, spinning the big sedan around in the courtyard and then taking off after Sanchez and his getaway driver.

I could see the rear lights up ahead, just a couple of hundred yards away, the Cadillac's headlamps on full beam leading the way. I accelerated off down the dirt track, trying to get the speed up without losing traction and making the wheels spin. I managed it better than the guy in front, and – combined with the extra power of the Mercedes – I started to gain on the Cadillac.

But I also knew what was coming up down the track – my own personal roadblock, courtesy of the stolen Honda SUV. I didn't want to get too close, or else I might be caught up in the ensuing crash.

Sure enough, it wasn't soon before I saw it, caught in the glare of the Cadillac's lights – the Honda, placed sideways across the end of the track, giving the lead car nowhere to go. Would the driver slam on the brakes? Veer off into the scrubland? Try and smash straight through it?

I let off the accelerator slightly, waiting to see what happened, one hand on the wheel while the other reflexively sought out the AR15, its presence reassuring.

My answer came soon enough – I heard the engine dip, then the revs increase, and I knew Sanchez had given the order to ram the Honda out of the way. I saw the Cadillac steam ahead, aiming slightly toward the right, obviously with the intention of clipping the front of the car, much smaller than the rear.

The only trouble was that – despite being visibly smaller – the front was where the engine block was housed, all six hundred pounds of it; he'd probably have been better off aiming for the back-end.

The impact came moments later, a colossal clash of metal on metal. The SUV was spun out of the way, and for a second I thought the Cadillac would make it, that I'd have to race off after it to try and take it down on the main road beyond; but then the big sedan veered right, its steering damaged.

In conjunction with the tire I'd shot out, the driver was losing all control, and the car was off the track altogether now, still going fast as it struck a small but evidently sturdy clump of Manzanita bushes.

This impact had an even more devastating effect than my two-ton SUV had done – the Cadillac was speared upward, front end coming off the ground, wheels still driving forward and propelling the vehicle up and over into a wild swing that put the car on its side, before crashing down onto its roof.

Seconds later I was pulling the Mercedes over, out and with the AR15 up and ready, approaching the broken Cadillac quickly but with due caution; the men inside were still armed, and potentially still capable of firing back.

I let off a burst at the upside-down rear, checking for the reaction. No shots came back my way, and I approached steadily, hunched down as I reached the cabin.

Through the broken glass, I saw the driver, blood leaking from facial wounds, trying to reach for his weapon in what seemed like slow motion, probably brought on by internal injuries. I gave him a blast of .223 and put him out of his misery permanently, before turning my attentions to Sanchez.

The leader of the Los Zetas sicarios was unconscious, blood leaking from one ear. I would have to grab him and pull him out of the car, just in case there was some sort of explosion. I couldn't question the man if he was burnt to a crisp.

I leaned in over the driver and turned the ignition off; and in that moment of distraction, Sanchez pulled out his pearl-handled pistol, eyes opening as it arced toward me.

He'd been playing possum all along, and had the drop on me; but my body reacted before my mind had the chance, and I knocked his gun arm to the side, the .45 slug blowing out the rear side window, deafening in the enclosed space. Letting my rifle dangle free on its sling, I kept hold of Sanchez's gun arm and reached further inside, grabbing the man by his long hair and slamming his face off the hard plastic dashboard.

He pulled back, dazed, and I picked up my rifle, held it back, and sent the butt straight into his temple, knocking him well and truly out for the count.

I went around to the passenger door, opened it and dragged Sanchez's unconscious body out of the crippled vehicle, pulling it across the dirty scrub toward the Mercedes. He was short but heavy, and the job took longer than I'd hoped; by the time we reached the trunk, I could already hear sirens far off in the distance, presumably drawn by reports of gunfire. We might have got away with it back up at the abandoned farm, but here – so close to the main road, and more inhabited areas – the sound of automatic weapons being used would have certainly drawn unwelcome attention. Hell, Sanchez might even have called the cops himself as he was driven down here.

I realized he might also have called a few more of his own boys too, and knew that the area would soon be crawling with people wanting to beat, kill or arrest me, and maybe all three. There was no use in going back up to the slaughterhouse to question Sanchez now; our privacy there was about to be terminally disrupted. I would just have to find somewhere else for our little chat, and I already thought that I knew where that would be.

I opened the trunk of the Mercedes, heaved

Sanchez up and over the lip, slammed it shut and hustled round to the driver's seat.

I pulled carefully around the broken Honda, traveled down to the junction with the main road, and pulled out smoothly, accelerating off as quickly as I dared.

I watched as three cop cars raced past me in the opposite direction, sirens blaring and lights flashing wildly, and breathed a sigh of relief.

I'd accomplished one part of that night's mission – I'd taken possession of Miguel Ángel Sanchez, the man Santiago had taken Elena Rosales to see three years, two months and five days ago.

And now all I had to do was find out what he remembered about it.

Chapter Nine

I watched as the man gagged, convulsed, shuddered, his entire body wanting to shut down but at the same time struggling desperately to breathe, to survive.

I stopped pouring the water from the bucket, put it down on the floor and monitored the effect the latest dousing was having on Sanchez.

Waterboarding has been used for centuries, although the actual term was only first officially used by the media in 2004. "Water board torture" was used to train US Navy recruits back in the 70s, and I remember undergoing the same thing myself with the RRD prior to deploying to Iraq in 2003. Despite the media's late uptake, we already knew it as waterboarding. It was nasty to be on the receiving end, but it was effective and – compared to many other forms of torture – relatively benign. The CIA, in fact, liked to refer to it as a "enhanced interrogation technique" rather than "torture".

And let's face it – who wouldn't rather undergo waterboarding than having electrodes on the testicles, fingernails pulled out, digits cut off, or any of the other horrendous, painful treatments that had been meted out over the years? I knew that Sanchez and his boys liked the bloody stuff, and I felt no guilt whatsoever about what I was doing to him. He'd certainly done a lot worse over the years, and had supposedly enjoyed it too.

Claims have been made about the long-term psychological effects of the technique, which is essentially designed to make the recipient think they are drowning, but – having experienced it myself – I have to call "bullshit" on that one. There are much worse things in life.

But the effect of the technique is immediate – you do actually feel as if you are drowning, which at the time is terrifying. You're ready to give up whatever you've got within the first half dozen dousings, often less.

So – maximal effect, minimal damage.

What's not to like?

It's also easy to set up, as my little interrogation center proved.

All you really need, other than the water itself, is a flat surface – ideally tilted at an angle of ten to twenty degrees, but horizontal will do just fine if that's all you've got; a way of securing the recipient; a piece of thin cloth to cover the face; and a dispenser for the water. In other words – the floor, a bit of rope, a towel and a bucket of water.

I had all these things, and a secure space too, out of the way of prying eyes and ears.

Sanchez and I were ensconced within a large metal shipping container, held within the large acreage of Quetzalcoatl International Airport. We were near the airport's public parking lot, where I'd left the Mercedes, in the yard of a big trucking firm called Transportes Fema.

The yard was covered in metal containers, literally hundreds of the things, and – with the airport only operating between eight in the morning and eight at night – the site was relatively empty; certainly enough for me to move around unmolested.

I'd left Sanchez in the car while I'd checked out the containers, selecting one well into the middle, surrounded by others to help cancel out any noise we might be making. I'd picked up supplies from an empty janitor's office, and returned to the car to get Sanchez.

I'd used rope to secure his arms and legs, tying the ends off on the conveniently located floor hooks – normally used for cargo ties to stop packing-crates from sliding around, but eminently suited for their new role. There hadn't been the means immediately available to angle him, but lying flat would still work just fine.

Performing the routine single-handed wasn't easy though – you had to secure the cloth to the face at the same time as you poured the water – but where there was a will, there was a way.

I wrapped the towel around his face and tied it off

at the back of his head, meaning I had my hands free to monitor the water flow. He thrashed and thrashed as I gave him another dose, but the rope held his body in place, and he took the full effect.

I knew that – despite the logical centers of his mind telling him it wasn't so – he would believe he was drowning, and would be more than willing to carry on giving me information.

I'd already had quite a large part of his life history – to get our relationship off to a good start, I'd started with something easy – and knew enough about the man to feel no remorse about his fate.

He was a very, *very* bad person.

He'd evidently grown up on the streets of Ciudad Juárez, one of the most violent cities in the world, and had killed his first victim at the tender age of eleven. Raped his first victim at twelve. Tortured his first victim – by hacking off the hands and feet with a saw – at the age of thirteen.

That had been for the Juárez Cartel but – after getting a short-lived shot of national pride and serving in the Mexican army's special forces – he later went to work for Los Zetas, who recruited him for his professional military skills.

He soon became their number one sicario and – in his own words – he had since lost count of the number of people he had killed. Men, women and even children. Sometimes raped, sometimes tortured.

He'd set up training camps for the new breed of sicarios, and was now involved in recruitment and organization, although he still apparently enjoyed getting his feet wet on occasion, taking on some of the big hits himself.

He used and abused women in an almost hateful fashion, and was particularly scathing in his opinion of the sex workers brought up to Mexico from Guatemala, Honduras and El Salvador. He considered them less than human, and was not at all concerned whether they survived his "treatment".

Which brought me onto the next topic of conversation.

I pulled the towel from his face, watched as he spluttered and gagged, still thinking he was drowning.

"What can you tell me about Elena Rosales?" I asked.

He sputtered again, then groggily asked, "Who?"

It was a fair question – it had been three years ago, and a man like Sanchez had probably seen so many young girls come and go that he might very well not remember Elena. Indeed, he might never have even known her name.

And yet he *had* requested her; and she was an American citizen, unlike many of the others who had been unfortunate to cross his path.

I had the feeling that Sanchez *did* remember; or *would*, when I made my questions more specific. His mind would be reeling, it would be hard to think straight, and I needed to remember that, make things easy for him.

"Three years ago," I said. "Three years, two

months, and five days. You asked a man called Santiago Alvarez to bring you a girl called Elena Maria Rosales. Thirteen years old at the time, a US citizen from right over the border in Laredo. She'd been across a few times, partied here. Santiago dropped her off for you outside Eclipse nightclub. She was never seen again. Do you remember?"

Sanchez spluttered again, shook his head. "Yeah, of course I remember," he spat.

"Good," I said. "That's good." I paused, letting him recover slightly so he could become more lucid. "Is she alive?" I asked next.

"Of course she's fuckin' alive man, what the fuck? Why you wanna know about her, man?"

I breathed out slowly, fully.

The girl was alive.

I could only imagine how happy her parents would be at the news. But what state would she be in? What had she been doing for the past three years?

I almost dreaded asking the question.

"Why did you want her?" I asked.

"*Sicario*," he murmured, and I failed to understand what he meant.

"You wanted her for your sicarios?" I asked.

He shook his head, almost smiling. "Dumb mutherfucker," he drawled. "No, man, no. I wanted her to *be* a sicario."

My heart went numb, my brain frozen.

I had to instantly recalculate everything I'd thought. Sex worker, drug mule, murder victim – all of these I'd considered, and been willing to accept. What I'd never contemplated was that the girl had been recruited into the cartel as a paid assassin.

"Why?" I asked, half-dumb, mind still reeling.

"Who suspects a girl, eh? Nobody, man, nobody. I wanted a young girl for the stable, someone we could train up, be my little black widow. An American was perfect, we could send her either side of the border, do hits here and there, hide out on either side too."

I shook my head, still struggling to understand, to believe.

"So you did?" I asked. "You recruited her? Trained her?"

"Fuck yeah," Sanchez said with some element of pride. "Bitch has killed more fuckin' people than *time*, man."

So Elena had been alive all these years, and had even been crossing the border – presumably with her own passport – to do jobs. I felt sickened, knew that the Laredo police must have just ignored Emilio's pleas to investigate properly. Probably just put it down to another girl missing over the border, not wanted to waste resources on it. A few simple checks would have highlighted her border crossings, could have got her held at the bridge, returned to her family.

But, as they say, shit happens. What I needed to know was, what could I do about it now?

"Where is she?" I asked him.

"Not here," he said with a smile, and I knew it was time for another dousing; he'd evidently forgotten what drowning felt like.

I pulled the towel back over his face and – despite his protests – tipped the bucket up over his head, the water running down over the cloth, soaking through until the spasms came, the convulsions, the fear and the terror.

When I guessed he'd had enough, I put the bucket down and pulled down the cloth.

"Try again," I said. "Where is Elena Rosales?"

"Laredo," Sanchez said instantly, "she's in fuckin' Laredo, man."

"Here in Nuevo Laredo?" I asked for confirmation.

"No man, in Laredo, American Laredo, Texas."

Son of a bitch.

Here I was shooting up half of Mexico, and the girl I was looking for was back where I'd come from, where her parents were sitting worried about her right now.

"What's she doing there?" I asked.

"Laying low for a while," Sanchez said. "Killed one of the top cops here. Married, but she was fuckin' him, stabbed him in his own bed, twenty times right through his fuckin' heart."

I could hear the pride again, and my heart sank even lower.

If what he was saying was even partially true, what sort of person was I going to return to Emilio and Camila? Was she going to be capable of rehabilitation? Or was she already too far gone?

There was only one way to find out.

"Where in Laredo is she?" I asked. "Give me an

address."

I could see Sanchez was about to resist – despite his condition, he was obviously unwilling to give up his little "black widow" without a fight – but when I reached for the towel, he shut his eyes quickly and shook his head.

"Okay, okay," he said. "Country Club Drive man, she's up on Country Club Drive."

"Nice place," I said.

"Yeah, we got a place there, nobody suspects who we got living there, it's funny, you know? Sicarios hanging out with the big shots, they got no idea who they are, they –"

But I was already pulling the towel back over Sanchez's face, dousing him with the water; I asked him again, just to make sure he'd not been lying the first time; and then I put the towel back on and this time kept it on, tight; so tight that Miguel Ángel Sanchez could no longer breathe at all.

He struggled against the ropes, against the cloth, but he was too tired, too weak; and eventually, he was just too *dead*.

The world would be one hell of a lot better off without him.

I rose, stretched my limbs, and assessed my next plan of action.

It seemed that my Mexican adventure was at an end.

It was time to go back home.

PART FOUR

Chapter One

Kane licked my face happily, glad to see me. I almost licked him back, but settled on giving his face and ears a good rub with my hands instead.

It had only been a couple of days, but what days they'd been. Kane offered a pleasant sense of normality, and I was glad to see him too.

But the job was far from over; I had information, yes. But I still had to act upon it.

I'd traveled back the night before, the way thousands of Mexicans had before me – swimming across the Rio Grande.

With my fake passport abandoned back in the hotel room, and my fake driver's license taken by the cops, I had no way of getting back into the US officially. Besides which, I had no idea if the Mexican police had put out some sort of warning for me; even if I'd had ID, it would have been a mistake to try and cross the border via US Immigration and Customs.

And so, after I'd finished with Sanchez, I'd taken another car and driven east toward the river, finally leaving the stolen vehicle on a quiet road near a large water treatment plant which nestled by the river.

Under cover of darkness, I'd made my way around the plant on foot, and slipped from the grassy banks of Mexico into the fast-flowing river.

As well as ICE border patrol agents, the Rio Grande was also patrolled by heavily armed gunboats from the Texas Department of Public Safety. But they weren't set up for covering every square inch of the huge river, especially at night, and it didn't take much to take advantage of gaps in the security net.

The river itself was a different story though, and the swim had been far from easy, the waters fast and with a vicious undercurrent that had threatened to pull me under every few seconds. And with every stroke I made, every foot of progress across the river, I was swept ten feet downriver, until – by the time I emerged, soaking wet and exhausted, on the other side, I was almost half a mile south from where I'd started.

But I was safe, far from the prying eyes of the border patrols, and I quickly collected myself and made my way north toward Laredo. The countryside here was the same as it was by the farm, dirty scrubland, open and barren. In the daylight, cover would have been hard to come by; but in the early morning hours, with the sun only just threatening to rise on the distant horizon, the dark welcomed me into its cloak of anonymity.

I'd called Emilio Rosales collect, had him come and pick me up from a minor road connecting to the main Zapata Highway which led back up into the city. If I'd walked, the sun would have come up on me and anyone who was around would see my wet clothes and jump to conclusions which – in this case at least – would be absolutely correct. The only people who would be hiking north up the highway, soaking wet on a bone-dry summer's morning, would be those who had just swam across the Rio Grande.

It would have been the same with hitch-hiking – I would have no way of knowing which drivers were pro-illegal entry, and which were against it. In general, however, most people were pretty strongly against it, which stacked the odds against me a little too much for comfort.

Calling Emilio was the safest thing to do, and within half an hour of the man picking me up, I was safely ensconced back in the family apartment on Salinas Avenue, Kane happily licking my hand while Emilio and Camila looked at me expectantly. I'd showered and changed and felt – almost – like a new man.

I hadn't discussed what I'd found out with Emilio during our drive here, telling him I needed to tell his wife at the same time. I'd told him she was still alive – it would have been unfair to hold out on him with that – but no more.

My reticence was less about wanting to wait to tell

175

Camila at the same time though, and more to do with the fact that I hadn't really decided what I was going to tell them.

"So she is alive?" Emilio asked, his wife's hand in his, looks of expectant hope on their faces.

I managed a smile. "Yes," I said. "Your daughter's alive."

"You've seen her?" asked Camila, the first time I had heard her speak. Her voice was full of excitement.

What do I tell them?

I shook my head. "No," I said. "I've not seen her. Not yet."

"What is wrong?" Camila asked. "You do not look happy about it. Why?"

I still didn't know what to say, and looked at my watch instead. It was just after half five in the morning. Full daylight outside, but still early for most people; maybe even for whoever was in that house on Country Club Drive.

I was running out of time; Sanchez was dead, and word would be out soon. If the safe house was alerted, who knew what the people there might do. If they freaked out and made a run for it, I might never have a chance of locating Elena again.

Ignoring the woman's question, I stood, my mind made up. I'd find Elena, see what sort of a state she was in, if she even *was* still Elena somewhere deep inside, and then I would decide how to handle things.

"I'm sorry," I said. "I need to go. I can't answer your questions right now, but we'll have this whole thing wrapped up soon, and then you'll know everything. But right now, I've got to move."

I strode for the door, Kane by my side, and didn't look back.

We had work to do.

CHAPTER TWO

I swung by the train station first to get my gear; there were a few things in my trusty backpack that I just might need. I pulled out a worn combat jacket and pocketed some choice items. I left the pack itself, as it would just weigh me down.

Then Kane and I ran north toward the safe house, six miles in forty-five minutes. I didn't want Emilio to drive me there, as I didn't want him to know where I was going; and if things worked out badly, I didn't want taxi or bus drivers to remember my route. Out for a run with my dog, nobody would give me a second look – especially at this time, when most people were still curled up in bed.

The time wasn't my best – in my younger days, back in the Rangers, I'd managed the distance in just shy of thirty-four minutes – but that had been on a track, and without the heavy jacket which was now weighing me down. Kane, not even breathing hard, still regarded me with disappointment in his eyes. He was a hard dog to impress.

It was still before half six, and the streets had yet to come alive. In fact the only people I'd seen so far – in this exclusive enclave of Laredo, far removed from the rougher neighborhoods further south – were maids and house workers on their way to clean up and make breakfast for their wealthy employers. How the other half lived.

It was, in fact, a different world up here, multi-million dollar villas spread through the neighborhood in huge lots, hundred thousand dollar cars parked in each driveway. Salinas Avenue it wasn't; and it was even further away from the blood-soaked mean streets of Nuevo Laredo.

And yet a part of Nuevo Laredo had come across the border and was infesting the area; one of the nearby houses bought with drug money, to provide a safe retreat and some R&R for the stone-cold cartel assassins.

Before killing Sanchez, when confirming his story about the safe house, I'd asked him how many others were hiding out there except for Elena. He'd told me four others, and I had no reason to doubt him. There were another two men stationed there permanently, but they weren't sicarios, they just looked after the place for the cartel "guests".

So, seven possibles, including Elena Rosales – or

Z13, as she'd become known since leaving home.

The first commander of Los Zetas – Arturo Guzmán Decena – had been known as Z1, after his Federal Judicial Police radio code; a code reserved for high-ranking officers. This was where the gang's name itself came from – "the Z's" – and many members had since taken on Z-numbers as their cartel names.

Elena was referred to as Z13, as that was the age at which she'd reportedly made her first kill. She'd been just thirteen years old.

As I made my way along the tree-lined avenues leading to Country Club Drive, I wondered how much there was left of the little girl who was still loved so much by her parents. Would there be any left at all?

Well, I supposed, I would find out soon enough.

I was almost there.

CHAPTER THREE

Laredo obviously wasn't as destitute a place as I'd first imagined; if the Country Club, with its golf course and tennis courts, was anything to go by, then some of its fair citizens must have been doing well there.

The houses on Palmer Drive backed up onto the golf course, their back yards looking out across the fairways. Kane and I had slowed to a walk now, taking in the world around us with every step. The target house was coming up soon, and all of my senses were perfectly attuned to the environment. And from the slight tension in Kane's body next to me, I knew his were, too.

With my combat jacket and utility pants I didn't exactly fit into these lustrous surroundings; but then again, I might well have been the hired help, out walking the rich owner's doggy. And anyway, there still wasn't anyone up and about to see me in the first place.

The houses all sat within enclosed lots, with plenty of fences and walls to keep the undesirables out. I could see the roof of the cartel safe house now, terracotta tiles already reflecting the warm light of the morning sun.

Closer now, and I could see that trees obscured much of the frontage; but it was a big place, low and wide, white stucco walls underneath the terracotta roof, set well back from the street.

Hidden.

Secure.

Maybe.

I half-expected dogs, but couldn't see any sign. Probably on account of the neighbors; if they wanted to keep a low profile, then a pack of barking pit bulls probably wasn't the best way of going about it.

No, I thought, anonymity was their best protection here; if nobody knew they were here, there would be nothing to worry about. And if anyone was foolish enough to trespass, then the villa's guests were trained sicarios, hardened killers.

I wondered what they got up to here, how good they were at keeping a low profile. I wondered if – after the action, the adrenaline, the fear, the excitement – they didn't find the luxury home a little boring after a while.

Kane and I were walking past the house now, on the other side of the road, eyes not directly on the place but at the same time still taking everything in.

There was movement somewhere in the front yard, and I focused for a split second to check what it was – a gardener, half-hidden in the trees.

But almost certainly *not* a gardener – probably one of the two gang members stationed permanently at the house, on perimeter guard duty. He might have clocked me, but it wasn't too troubling – he'd have no more reason to suspect me than anyone else.

But then again, I considered, my presence might set alarm bells ringing – if he habitually frequented the front yard, he *might* think it strange that he'd never seen me before.

Well, I thought, *shit*.

I was tight for time anyway.

Might as well take the bull by the horns.

I adjusted my position, eyes alighting fully on the small Latino man in the yard, making it clear that I'd seen him, and trotted over the road with Kane right by my side.

"Good morning," I said with a wave as I came closer. "I just moved in down the street, just out exploring the neighborhood."

The man looked up from where he'd been pretending to dig out weeds from around the trees and bushes – or actually *had* been digging, I could see now – but otherwise ignored me. I wondered how long that would last.

I reached the gate, noting how thick the ironwork was, how the fence reached just a little bit higher than those of the surrounding properties; not enough to stand out or draw attention to itself, but enough to make a difference if you wanted to attack the place. It would make it just that little bit harder.

"My name's Tom," I continued with a smile, face up against the gate now. "Tom Dalby. I wasn't really expecting anyone to be around at this time, you must be a really early bird like me, huh?"

The man's eyes fixed on mine. They were pure black, death behind them. He was small, but with a wiry muscularity that screamed *predator*.

"Which house have you moved into?" the man asked in broken English.

"Eleven forty-two," I answered. "Real nice around here." I looked down at myself sheepishly. "I should probably get myself some new clothes, but I've come from Detroit and it's cold as hell up there, you know?"

"Eleven forty-two wasn't for sale," the man said, suspicion in his eyes now, body tensing, ready for action.

"I never said I bought it," I said quickly. "House swap with Dennis and Jean for the season, you know?" I hoped he wouldn't know the first names of the people who lived at eleven forty-two; I'd selected the number as it was a long way down the street, and I assumed the man's knowledge of its residents would be limited, if it existed at all. "Heat gets a bit much for them in the summer down here," I continued, "my place is on a lake and they're gonna get some fishing in, cool down a bit. You know how they are, right?"

He nodded his head, tried to smile. He had a tough role to play – on the one hand, he needed to be suspicious, to guard his own safe house; on the other, he had to appear normal and at least half-friendly, so as not to attract suspicion to himself.

"Yes," he said, "they do like their fishing."

It was as I thought; he knew there hadn't been a for-sale sign in the lot, but he had no idea who really lived there.

"Anyway," I said, "I promised to look after their yard while they were gone, and I'm not really that much into gardening. Do you know anyone who looks after yards?"

He shook his head, and as he did so, I saw movement at one of the windows behind him. It seemed someone else was also up and around in there, and time really *was* running out.

"I'm sorry," he said. "As you can see, I take care of my own, I don't really have any details for gardeners."

"Okay," I said, "no problem. Can I give you my card? That way, if you hear anything, you can give me a call."

I already had the card out, in my hand – it was a business card for a taxi firm that we'd used when we'd gone out for drinks in Laredo a few nights before, but that wouldn't matter for long – and held it out for him, putting it in between the bars of the iron gate that still stood between us.

I could see the conflict in his eyes – the lack of trust, at odds with the desire to seem normal, to not refuse the gesture I'd made.

In the end, social propriety – and his desire to not seem out of the ordinary himself – won the day, and he extended his hand to the gate, accepting the card.

As he made contact, my other hand shot out through the bars, grabbing hold of his shirt and pulling him violently toward me.

His face hit the metal bars at high velocity, the impact shaking him; but although his knees sagged, his eyes were still open and I released slightly before pulling him in again, his skull hitting this time, the impact even harder.

The man went down, out for the count, and I immediately pulled the keys from his belt that I'd seen when he was walking toward me, instinctively selecting the one I thought would make the best fit with the gate's lock.

It worked, and the gate swung open; I slipped in, closing it behind me and pulling the man's unconscious body into the tree line to hide it from view. I checked the man's pockets and found a wallet, a lock knife, and a Beretta 9mm.

The trees that made the house nearly invisible from the street also meant that – from a security standpoint – anyone watching from inside would also be at a disadvantage, as they couldn't see the approach of an intruder.

I took full advantage of that now, pistol in my hand as I tracked through the trees toward the front door.

As I got nearer, Kane still at my side – his body keyed up on adrenaline, just like mine – I withdrew the FN pistol from the pocket of my combat jacket. I'd brought it with me across the river from Nuevo Laredo, never having had the chance to use it back at the abandoned farm.

A weapon in each hand – the FN in my right as it was lighter and my arm still wasn't a hundred percent from the icepick incident – I concentrated on controlling my breathing as I approached the door, centering myself for the task ahead.

I hadn't used the FN at the farm perhaps, but I was sure as hell going to use it now.

I left the safety of the trees, slipped across the brick driveway to the porch, and crept up the two small steps that led to the door.

"Wait here," I told Kane with a nod of my head. "You know what to do."

Kane sat to the side of the door, waiting with anticipation for what was to come.

Because even he knew that all freaking hell was about to be let loose.

CHAPTER FOUR

I knew the door would be open – the man outside would need quick access in case of trouble, and the people inside would also need to be able to escape quickly, through the front or the back.

I therefore put my hand on the handle, turned, and eased the big oak door open, my footsteps silent as I crossed the threshold.

Subtlety didn't last long though – a face appeared across the hall, and disappeared just as quickly; the figure I'd seen moving about from the street.

The face reappeared moments later – the body hidden behind a rattan sofa – along with a burst of fire from a suppressed MAC-10 machine pistol. The suppressor reduced the terrifying noise, but that wasn't its only job – it also made the weapon easier to control on full-auto, as it discharged twelve hundred rounds a

THE THOUSAND DOLLAR MAN

minute, twenty rounds per second.

But despite the aid, controlling the little beast was still awkward at best – at that rate of fire, the entire magazine was discharged in just one and a half seconds, most of them up toward the ceiling.

I ducked low and aimed high, firing two shots from the FN that hit the gunman straight in the exposed face, a bright red spray of blood covering the sofa he'd been hiding behind.

Noise caught my attention from the left and I pivoted, seeing a half-naked man – tattoos covering his muscular body – charging down the stairs, an oversized Smith and Wesson revolver in his hands. From the huge hole at the end of the six-inch stainless-steel barrel, I knew it must have been the .50 caliber version – overkill for a handgun if ever there was one, it would have put Dirty Harry's to shame. The thing could take down a rampaging rhino.

He fired it on the move and I dodged again, hunkering down as the colossal rounds whizzed over my head, taking out half of the wall behind me.

The entire hacienda was erupting now, shouts and screams in Spanish from both lower and upper floors, everyone in the house aware now of what was going on.

Who would escape, and who would stay and fight?

It only occurred to me at that point that if Elena – sicario that she was – attacked me, I might end up killing her.

And what would I tell her parents then?

But it was time to move, not to think, and I

bounced up momentarily, acquiring a sight picture for the man with the .50 and letting loose with rounds of my own.

Two shots hit him from the FN, one from the Beretta, and the big man went down hard; but there was no time to gloat, and I was already turning again, firing instinctively as I saw a man with a heavily scarred, pockmarked face racing toward me, carving knife in hand.

I shot him with the Beretta, one in the chest and one in the throat as the muzzle lifted slightly.

Four down, three – including Elena Rosales – left to go.

I had a decision to make – should I clear the entire lower floor before heading upstairs, or should I assume that the others had been sleeping, and would more likely be upstairs, in which case a full search of the lower floor might give them chance to regroup, arm themselves properly, or escape?

I tracked toward the stairs, not wanting to take the chance of Elena escaping; but when I was halfway up, I saw movement from below, a man running for the front door. Unarmed, and obviously wanting to get the hell out of there.

Guess I'd been wrong about everyone being upstairs.

But the next thing I heard were terrified screams from outside, and I knew Kane would have stopped the man in his tracks. He wouldn't kill the man if he was unarmed, but he would take him to the ground,

Shutzhund-style, and keep him pinned to the floor with jaws around his neck.

I took the stairs slowly now, all too aware that it was easier to fight down than to fight up. Both pistols were aimed up the stairwell, fingers on the triggers.

But then something came hurtling toward me, out of nowhere, hitting me full in the chest and knocking me backwards, head angled toward the floor as I slid down the stairs on my back, each step banging into my spine, guns dropping uselessly to the floor.

I'd been hit by a man, even bigger than the one with the .50, and I realized he must have jumped over the bannister, from the landing above; I felt him on top of me as we slid down the stairs, saw his wild eyes just inches from mine, felt his huge hands going around my throat.

We hit ground level, the back of my head striking the hard tiled surface and making me see stars, brain dizzy, my equilibrium gone; and still the huge man was on top of me, hands wrapped around my neck and squeezing hard.

I heard something from the side, a big splash, and turned my head slightly to see what it was. Through the fog of strangulation, I saw a big pair of French doors leading to the rear yard, golf course beyond. In that yard was a swimming pool.

And in that swimming pool, a young woman was swimming frantically to the side, having obviously just jumped in from the upper floor window.

Elena Rosales.

She was getting away.

My knee lifted sharply into the gorilla's balls, without much effect; and so I took the little finger of one of the hands which was wrapped around my throat, pulled it away from the rest, and twisted it sharply.

It snapped like a twig, and the big man screamed out in pain; my knee shot up into the balls again and this time – not able to tense for it – he bucked with the impact, body weakened momentarily. The hands softened around my neck and I used the opportunity, driving my own arms up between his, thumbs raking across his eyes.

He cried out in pain again, and I threw him off me, regaining my feet; the big man wasn't dead, but I didn't have to kill *everybody* I met. Besides which, he was well and truly out of action, and I had a runaway teenage sicario to catch.

I started off at a sprint toward the French doors, hands out to open them, and then I felt the impact – a huge, bone-shaking impact that knocked the breath right out of me.

The big guy, damaged but evidently not out for the count, had decided to go another round, and had tackled me hard from behind, driving me toward . . .

The glass doors shattered outward as the huge sicario slammed me right through them, the shards cutting my hands, my face; and still he kept on propelling me forward across the stone-slabbed terrace, my body still unable to breathe, unable to resist.

We hit the pool together, his weight driving me

under, and the cool water served to bring me around, to make me react.

My body twisted under the water, turning into him, hands now around his throat. I saw his damaged eyes go wide in panic, and I released slightly; and in his desperation to breathe, he opened his mouth wide, taking a huge gulp of pool water right into his lungs.

He coughed, spluttered, gagged, and panicked once more, mouth opening and taking in even more water; but his hands reached out and grabbed me, vice-like in a death grip. I tried to keep him under, but his survival instincts were too strong, and he propelled us both to the surface.

As our heads breached the churning water, we both took in great lungfuls of sweet, precious air; but I recovered moments before he did, and fired the edge of my hand into his throat in an oblique, chopping action. I could have sworn I heard the trachea snap, cartilage destroyed; but then I felt the beast's hands grip me again, still possessed by ferocious strength, and he rammed me into the concrete side of the pool.

The impact was hard, driving the breath from me once again; and as I coughed in pain, I saw the girl, dripping wet, running for the rear fence that led to the Laredo Country Club beyond.

It was now or never – she would soon be away, never to be seen again – but the guy was so strong I wasn't sure what else I could do, how I could beat him.

It was then I spotted it, out of the corner of my blurred, deteriorating vision; and reflexively my hand sought it out and put it into action.

The hosepipe snaked around the man's thick, bulging neck, my hands wrapping it around again and again and again, pulling it tight until his hands left my body and went to try and pull the rubber garrote away; and it was then that I pushed away from the side of the pool with my feet, dropping low under the water and pulling down on the pipe, dragging the man under with me by his neck, his hands still frantically grabbing at it, trying to pull it off. But it was too tight, and he could no longer fight it; with his throat already damaged by my blow, the man's breathing capacity already restricted, the hosepipe did its job quickly; the man jerked violently, but I held him tight until his eyes went wide, almost as if they would jump out of his head; and then he relaxed completely, body floating lifelessly in the water.

I burst to the surface again, just in time to see Elena's legs disappear over the fence.

I sighed as I pulled myself out, resigned to more hard work.

The chase was on.

CHAPTER FIVE

I vaulted the fence in one smooth movement, saw the girl sprinting away over the fairway, just seventy yards ahead of me; then heard the sound of gunshots, felt the hot sparks as bullets hit the metal fence around me.

I looked back through the fence, saw two men running from the house, firing their AR15s on full-auto. I cursed myself for my stupidity – just because I knew about the potential of seven people being in the house didn't mean that there weren't more. Friends, colleagues, guests, it didn't matter; what did matter was that as soon as they vaulted that fence, they would have a nice clear line of fire toward me, no matter how far I managed to run.

I'd dropped my guns back in the house but, without even thinking, I felt my hands scoop into the pockets of my combat jacket, fractions of a second later coming back out, throwing what was in them hard and fast toward the men racing after me.

The ten-inch carbon-steel Smith and Wesson military-grade throwing knives spun through the air, one after the other after the other, aimed through the bars of the fence.

The first hit one of the guys straight in the face, making the AR15 arc up high, firing to the sky; the next hit him in the chest and dropped him to the floor. As he was falling, the second man – obviously well-trained – tried to dodge to the side; but it was too little, too late, and the third knife hit him in the shoulder, the fourth – slightly adjusted – directly in the middle of the chest.

The assault rifles were silent now, the only sound the blood bubbling up from the men's wounds, coughed violently from their mouths.

I turned my attentions back to the fairway, saw Elena a hundred yards away, racing around the huge pond that provided a water hazard for the club's golfers. I saw residential houses on the other side, a network of streets. If she made it around, I might lose her.

There were other people on the course now, groundskeepers and caretakers, all coming to have a look at where the gunshots had been coming from, now surprised and shocked to see two random, soaking wet people charging across their well-kept lawns.

Legs pumping, heart racing wildly, I felt myself gaining on the girl – now just eighty yards away.

Of course, I realized what it must have looked like to the people watching – big scary man chasing after small teenage girl.

Not good for me.

By this time, there were even people out in their yards, or else watching from the windows of their palatial homes. I knew several people would have called the police already.

Police headquarters was not even five miles away – with a high alert, they could be here within eight minutes, or as little as five, depending on how they were driving; and if there were patrols close to the area, they could be here even sooner than that.

Shit.

I increased my pace, stride opening, eating up the yards.

I saw the men rushing toward me across the green, three of them, all obviously wanting to save the girl from the scary man.

Others were racing toward the girl, presumably to try and protect her.

I couldn't blame them, of course; I would have done the same in their shoes.

But I also couldn't allow them to slow me down.

Just forty yards left between us.

So close.

The men tried to tackle me from the side, and I sidestepped one in good football style, his bodyweight carrying him on forward into the pond; the next got an elbow jerked sideways into his face that dropped him to the lawn, and I pulled the third down by his ears and just stepped on top of him, jumping forward off his prone body and carrying on running.

Thirty yards, and the girl was nearing the edge of the water, where it curved toward the housing. A small crowd waited for her, to welcome her into their protection.

Twenty yards, and I heard the first sirens, saw four men approach me.

Ten yards and we met, the girl now within the protection of four earnest, well-meaning women.

I punched the first man on the chin, our bodyweights moving together to create knockout power, and he fell motionless to the ground. I kicked out sideways at another, taking the wind out of his sails; grabbed another, planted my forehead into his face; then round kicked the last man in the thigh, my hardened shin smacking straight into the nerve cluster and dropping him to the ground.

I saw Elena's face then for the first time – so young, and yet at the same time so very, very old; she'd seen things that nobody should have seen, at any age, and it had left her scarred in more ways than one. Tattoos lined her face and – though she had once no doubt been pretty – it seemed that Z13 had all but taken over, and Elena was almost gone.

Her face registered the horror of my arrival, and I could see her nervous, animal eyes running through tactics; and with the sirens sounding ever louder, she made her choice.

She wouldn't know I was there to save her, would assume that I'd come to kill her; and why would she think any different? Even if I told her, she would never believe me.

She grabbed one of the women who'd been helping her, arm going around her throat while her other hand pulled out a wicked-looking serrated blade from a hidden pocket, holding it up against the victim's neck.

The speed was incredible, one of the fastest draws I'd ever seen; and the look on the girl's eyes made me think she had exactly what was needed to execute this woman in cold blood, and then go right onto another.

The other women stood there in shock, unable to compute the situation, to reconcile the fact that the young girl they were trying to help was now holding a knife to the throat of their friend.

The police would be here any minute and – while it wouldn't be so bad if they arrested Elena Rosales – I sure as hell didn't want to be taken into custody. Too many questions, too many unsavory answers.

And on second thoughts, I didn't really want Elena to be arrested, at least not yet, not before I'd verified that there was an Elena still in there somewhere. I wanted to bring Emilio's daughter back, not the empty shell that was Z13.

"Back the fuck up, mano!" the girl screamed, her voice high, the intention behind it violent. "Back up or I split this bitch's throat right open!"

Her eyes were wide, and I had no doubt whatsoever that she would carry out the threat, then go onto someone else.

I knew I was running out of time, the cops would

descend on the place any second.

Z13 started to back away, past the other women, heading through the rear yard of the house for the open street on the other side of the property.

"Get me a fucking car," she shouted to the small crowd, "right fucking now!"

The knife pressed deeper into the soft skin of her hostage's neck, and the women started to move, pulling out keys or rushing back to their houses.

"I'm leavin' here, mano," she told me. "I'm fuckin' leavin'."

"In that?" I asked, my eyes roaming to the left, and the sound of a car being started up.

It was the oldest trick in the book, but her desperation for transport out of there made her fall for it, her eyes moving for a moment – just a moment – to the source of the noise, to confirm that a vehicle was on its way as she'd demanded.

That moment was all I needed.

In the blink of an eye, I whipped out a heavy, wooden-handled Bowie knife and hurled it through the hot morning air.

It was thrown quickly, fluidly, but – in the time-distortion of adrenaline – it seemed to turn over and over itself in slow motion, each rotation reflecting sunlight off the gleaming blade.

But then it reached the target and made impact, just before her eyes snapped forward again.

The heavy hilt of the knife, butt-capped in solid brass, hit the girl square in the center of the forehead, causing shock and a momentary loss of ability to do anything except stand there, open mouthed.

I used that opportunity to rush forward, covering the last few yards between us in a frantic dash; and as I reached her, I snatched her knife away from her victim's throat, pushed the woman away from danger, and unleashed a heavy, open handed slap with my callused palm that struck the girl across the face and knocked her unconscious, the pain receptors in the large surface area of skin unable to process so much information and shutting her brain down, the whole system malfunctioning.

She dropped to the floor, but I was already next to her, catching her and scooping her into my arms as I raced past the house, heading for the street and the vehicle that I'd seen, one of the women having done as the girl had demanded and bringing her a car.

It was a little Mercedes two-seat sports car – fast, agile, and absolutely perfect. There was something to be said for money after all.

"Get out," I said, slinging Elena onto the passenger seat and sliding behind the wheel as the woman exited the car. Engine already on, I gunned the accelerator and raced off down the street, sirens sounding so close now that I knew the cops must be right on top of us.

But where there was a will, there was a way; and I sure as hell wasn't going to get caught now.

CHAPTER SIX

The little neighborhood was planted right smack in the middle of the country club grounds, and we were in a cul-de-sac with only one way out – straight ahead.

I accelerated that way, hurtling around the bends and heading east – if the golf course surrounded the oasis on the other three sides, as it appeared, then the link to the main roads would have to be east, and I made the decision and stuck to it.

Ignoring a turn-off to my right, I swept around the road, narrowly avoiding a couple of cars just setting off for work; and then I could see it up ahead – a junction to a main road, and my exit out of there.

But I could also see police cruisers heading down my way, and I instinctively eased off the accelerator, slowing the car to pretend I was just another white-collar worker on my way to the office.

The cruisers zipped past me, three of them; but a cop in the last car had looked across at me and made a connection in his trained mind. Perhaps it was the combat jacket, or the fact I was soaking wet; but something didn't gel with him, and he pulled up on the handbrake and made a perfect turn. My foot was stomping down on the accelerator before he could get back on his own, and I shot forward along the tree-lined avenue, heading for the main road ahead, at least one cop car right behind me.

The T-junction up ahead led either north or south; but I knew that more of the country club lay north and so wrenched the wheel to the right, spilling out of the avenue onto Bermuda Drive, accelerating even as I whipped the car around the other early-morning traffic.

I saw a sign for East Del Mar Boulevard, and piloted the vehicle in that direction, cop car right behind me. And I knew his friends wouldn't be far behind *him*; he'd also almost certainly been on the radio by now, called in the make and model of my vehicle and requested back-up to my location.

I took a left, sweeping down the last section of Bermuda Drive toward the intersection with Del Mar; and then we were there, the car ploughing out across the wide lanes, cars swerving around us, and I had to fight with the wheel to correct it, pull us straight; but then the car stabilized, the tires gripped, and we were off.

The sportster accelerated hard, the engine free-revving and potent, and we were up to eighty in no time at all, swerving in and out of the morning traffic and heading northwest, following signs for Loop 20, a four-lane highway that passed both Texas A&M University, and Laredo International Airport.

I was just sailing around a big camper van when I felt the hands raking out at my face, heard the feral screams.

Z13 was awake and angry.

Feeling terrible about it – but not wanting to crash the car and have us both killed – I reached over, gripping the wheel with one hand as we sped at eighty down the wide boulevard, grabbed hold of her hair, and ran her face straight into the dashboard.

The impact was hard, and the effect immediate – the girl was knocked out cold once more, hopefully for the duration.

It pained me to hit a woman – but being involved in a high-speed automobile crash would certainly have pained me a lot more. And I didn't much fancy having my eyes raked out either.

As we raced past JB Alexander High School on the right, I counted four sets of flashing sirens in my rear-view. But the Mercedes sports car was faster – and certainly more agile – and if I played my cards right, there was still a chance I could get out of there.

Not a *good* chance perhaps, but it was still a chance – and that was a whole lot better than nothing at all.

I could see the intersection coming up now, traffic busy on the Bob Bullock Loop, streaming past at fifty in both directions, four lanes apiece. Traffic lights, stop signs, and not a hell of a lot else over the other side of the highway, just desert scrubland.

I didn't slow down at all, just kept on accelerating into traffic exactly as I'd done onto Del Mar a few short minutes before; with no obstructions in the way I could see the road clearly, identify the vehicles, their positions, their speeds, calculate my speed and angle of approach so that I could meet the traffic seamlessly.

It worked, the little Mercedes bursting out right in front of a Ford sedan and immediately sprinting away from it, around two other slow-moving cars and out into a clear fast-lane, gunning the engine until we were running at over a hundred.

I knew the cop cars would be far behind us; but with radio comms and the possibility of helicopters, I knew we weren't out of the woods yet.

But luckily, I had a plan.

CHAPTER SEVEN

For the next mile I really pushed the little sportster, opening up as much distance between me and the cops as possible.

By the time I'd reached the turn-off for the university, I couldn't even see their flashing lights; and so I swung off, reducing my speed now so as not to get noticed by anyone that happened to be around. Not that university campuses at seven in the morning were normally hives of activity – most students probably wouldn't be anywhere near awake yet.

I drove through the pretty campus, full of modern white-walled and red-roofed buildings sat between manicured lawns and gardens, until I came to a parking lot.

I parked the Mercedes up in a shadowy corner, then took the opportunity to secure Elena's wrists and ankles with the duct tape I'd brought with me. I left her in the car while I approached the nearest vehicle, a small Mazda hatchback, and quickly broke into it. Acting as casually as I could – as if both vehicles were mine and I was simply transferring some luggage between the two – I went back to the Mercedes, lifted Elena from the passenger seat, and placed her in the trunk of the hatchback. She was starting to come round, but not enough to cause any problems.

I slammed the lid, took off my jacket and stuffed it down into the rear foot-well. It wasn't much, but it was one less thing to identify me by. I then slipped into the driver's seat, hotwired the engine, and pulled slowly out of the lot.

Above me I heard – and then saw – a helicopter, noted its Laredo PD markings, and wondered if they'd seen me switch cars.

But as I re-entered Loop 20, there didn't seem to be a rush of police cars toward me, and the chopper appeared to be just roaming in a random pattern.

It paid to be certain though, and so a couple of miles further south I turned in again, this time into the parking lot of Laredo International Airport. I knew the chopper wouldn't be able to fly over the area, and I would be able to change cars again relatively unmolested.

The switch took just a few minutes, and then – the girl once more secured in the trunk – I was leaving the airport and rejoining the Loop, this time in an ancient, lime-green GM sedan.

The chopper was still overhead, and I could still hear sirens all around me – sometimes even saw a police cruiser shoot past, lights flashing, horns blaring – but nobody seemed in the least interested in me or my ugly green car.

I'd done it; we were safe.

Now I just had to get Z13 somewhere we could talk, so I could assess just how much of Elena Rosales there was left inside before I presented her to Mom and Dad.

CHAPTER EIGHT

The sixteen-year-old sicario known in the Los Zetas underworld as Z13 eyed me warily across the room.

We were in a safe location, in Jeb Wilkins' old room at the downtown hostel; some of his things had yet to be collected, and nobody else had taken it over since his death. Perhaps someone would soon, but not yet; and for now, the place was about as safe as I could find.

I wasn't worried about Kane – he was used to the streets, and he would have hightailed it out of there long before the cops could have called in the pound to take him away. He would have headed back to Emilio's apartment, knowing that I would be likely to meet him there eventually.

The girl was still bound, and tied to a chair; she had yet to give me any reason to trust her, and until she did, she would stay right where she was.

She was a pretty girl, or perhaps had been, once upon a time. Her body was trim and athletic, hard and wiry like a fighter's. She was tattooed, most noticeably on her face. There were teardrops on her cheeks, and – when her eyes were closed – I was surprised to see eyeballs tattooed onto her eyelids. The effect was disturbing, to say the least.

Images of Santa Muerte, the "Saint of Death" – who was dreaded and revered throughout Mexico, especially by the cartels and their followers – adorned both her arms, and there was a series of straight lines around her neck, every four lines crossed through by a fifth. It looked like a prisoner had been counting the days of incarceration and marking them off on a cell wall; or an assassin commemorating her victims.

I didn't want to count them.

I noticed things other than wariness in the girl's eyes too – there was violence, anger, and also fear. There was the glazed, hopeless look of the addict as well, and I wondered if that wasn't partially how Sanchez had molded and controlled her.

"You want a fix?" I asked her.

"Fuck you," she said, before spitting on the threadbare carpet – but at my words I had seen a flicker of hope in those cold eyes, of need, and I knew she was a junkie; the next few hours – perhaps days – were definitely not going to be fun for her.

"Is that how it started?" I asked. "They got you hooked on that shit? Made you do it?"

She just looked at me, opening and closing those tattooed eyelids; the sight was unnerving.

"Let me tell you why you're here," I said. "Why *I'm* here. I was hired by your parents to find you." I paused to let that sink in. "I was hired to find Elena Maria Rosales, by a mom and dad who love that girl very much. So much so, that they've hardly slept in the past three years, lying awake at night and wondering what happened to their daughter, hoping and praying that she was okay."

I nodded my head. "Yeah, those parents have tried everything, the police, the media, even the damn FBI. But nobody could help them, and so they came to me. Their last chance."

I looked at her, searching for what lay beneath those hard eyes, what lay inside. "What am I going to tell them?" I asked. "Is their little girl already dead? Or is Elena Rosales still alive, still capable to returning to her family, to her normal life?"

"And who the fuck are *you?*" she asked – but although her words were fierce, a little of the fire, a little of the hardness, had gone out of those eyes; perhaps a little bit of Elena shining through the darkness.

"My name doesn't matter," I said. "All that matters is that your parents paid me a thousand dollars to find you."

She smirked. "The Thousand Dollar Man, eh? I heard about you, mano. Didn't think you was real, esse. But you fight like Santa Muerte man, hah! You a real tough motherfucker. What's your story?"

She was talking, and that was important; she wasn't giving me the evil eye any more. She might not exactly be opening up herself, but it was progress. I wanted her to trust me, so that we could get a real dialogue going. If I told her something, perhaps she would tell me something in return.

"My story?" I said. "It's a long one."

"We going somewhere, mano?"

"I guess not," I conceded, and stretched out my arms, rested back in my own chair. "It all started when I was injured, I suppose."

"Iraq?" she asked, and I nodded my head.

"Yeah, a battle just outside Mosul. Got shot to shit, most major bones broken, you know the score – not a great day at the office. Anyway, when I was finally discharged they gave me a payout but I gave it all away to the family of a friend of mine who was killed during that same battle. I promised him I'd look after his family, and that's just what I did.

"Still, it left me with nothing except an empty bank account and no real job prospects. Things are better now than they were after Vietnam, but who's really gonna hire an injured infantry veteran? I mean, what's my skill set? I can kill people, that's what I'm trained for. Tried running some martial arts classes for a while, but I guess I was still wound a bit tight from the war, took things a bit too seriously. Got a lot of students, but not many wanted to stick it out. *Relax*, they said, *there's no war going on here,* they said. But there was for me, the war was still going on inside and I couldn't stop it if I tried.

"Anyway, after a while I decided to roam around, look for work, taking anything I could get. I worked in bars and clubs as a bouncer, on construction sites as a bricklayer, I valeted cars for showrooms, grilled the meat at fast food joints. You name it, I did it. Kept applying for overseas security jobs, but was always turned down on medical grounds. Didn't matter a shit what I'd done over my career, only that in the end I'd gone out on a medical discharge. Nobody wanted to touch me, couldn't get insurance for me, they said. Couldn't take the risk.

"But then I was in North Carolina, heard they were doing a big recruitment drive at a slaughterhouse out at a place called Tar Heel. A real hole, but that processing plant was just about the biggest in the world, did over thirty thousand pig carcasses a *day*. Anyway, bottom line is that they hired me and I pulled twelve hour shifts cutting and hauling hundred-pound pig bodies for the next year and a half.

"I was still helping out my dead buddy's family, sending back some of my pay every month to them. Did a few extras on the side too, got involved in some pit fights to raise a bit of extra cash. You know, bare knuckle fights on the slaughterhouse floor, whole crews of guys watching and betting. They probably made more money out of it than I ever did.

"Found out that my friend's son – my godson – had leukemia right about then, I started fighting more, pulling extra shifts, sending even more money their way.

Saved a bit too, wanted to go and visit them up in Alaska. Hell of a long way, and a good chunk of dough to get there, you know? But things weren't looking good, and I wanted to see him. Poor kid was only about six years old." I shook my head. "No justice in the world."

I noticed that Z13 – Elena? – was sitting there quietly, listening to my every word. Had there even been a flicker of sympathy in her eyes when I'd mentioned the boy?

I wasn't making it up for her benefit though; it was a true story, and one which still threatened to bring a tear to my eye.

"It was the Mexicans that did it for me in the end," I continued. "Not their fault of course, they needed the work just like everyone else; but the company started shipping them in by the busload, illegal workers who could work for less money, put in longer hours, completely unregulated. The management loved it, of course. Immigration did raids, but the higher-ups always caught wind of it early and sent those workers off for the day. And if they ever *did* get caught, they would take their little fines, get rid of those guys and just ship across more from over the border. I mean they literally did just that, bused them over on a daily basis, round-trips of hundreds of miles. They saved millions, and how could American workers compete with that?

"A few of my buddies got canned, and I brought it up with one of the senior executives during a "shop floor" visit. He got in my face, told me my medals weren't worth shit, I should be grateful to be there, you know? So I got in his face and put him on his ass, broke the guy's jaw.

"And so they let me go too, what else could they do? They would have pressed charges, but they didn't want cops all over the place, didn't want their own operation looked at too closely.

"But it left me without a job, right when I really needed the money. I went out looking for work, day after day, but there was nothing, and every night I returned to my trailer empty-handed. The boy was getting worse up in Alaska too, and I knew I had to go and see him before it was too late.

"And then one day I got back home, and the place had been burglarized, totally emptied – including the money I'd saved to go and visit my godson, every last cent of it. A thousand dollars.

"Well, I guess that was the last straw, you know? I'd been beaten up and put upon for too damn long, and I wasn't going to take it anymore, not for one more fucking second.

"I made up my mind to get my money back, and that's what I set out to do. Spent a week looking for the lowlifes who'd hit my trailer, finally found them and put them in hospital for three months apiece. Sonsofbitches. Got my money back, plus plenty more besides.

"Went and got myself a ticket to Alaska right away, but by the time I got there, it was too late. My godson, my buddy's little boy, was dead. And I'd never got the chance to see him, to hold his hand, to be there instead of his own father. And all because of that lousy thousand dollars, and the bastards who'd stolen it.

"It was then that I knew what it was I was going to do with my life. It was like a miracle, Saint Paul on the road to Damascus, a revelation.

"I was made for war, and nothing else. It was in my blood, what I'd been trained for, what I was good at. And there was a war going on right here in America, from the scumbags who robbed me, to the big corporations pissing on the little people to make their own pile of money grow bigger and bigger. There was a war going on alright, and it was people like that, against people like me, like your mom and dad. Like Elena Rosales.

"And I stood over that little boy's body, and I vowed to fight that war, a thousand dollars at a time."

The girl was silent for a moment, then her face softened ever so slightly. "I'm sorry," she said.

I nodded my head, wiped the single tear from my cheek, and held her gaze.

"Well, that's my story," I said. "Now what's yours?"

CHAPTER NINE

To my surprise, the girl talked; and when she started, it was like she never wanted to stop.

Perhaps it shouldn't have surprised me; these were things she must have kept bottled up for all that time, nobody to share them with, only the prospect of death and pain ahead of her – either hers or someone else's.

The first part of her story tallied with what Noemi had told me. She'd been a quiet girl, yes; but with a rebellious spirit that Noemi had awakened, and which found its release across the bridge, on the excitement-fueled streets of Nuevo Laredo.

She'd smoked, she'd drank, and – without too much encouragement – she'd done drugs too. She'd not slept with her cousin Mateo but – at his direction – had certainly slept with plenty of his friends, including one Santiago Alvarado.

She'd fallen deeply in love with the low-level hood, been enticed by his bad-boy image, the way people deferred to him in the street. He was a *somebody*, a real man, and he wanted her. She didn't want anyone else, and it didn't even bother her that Noemi had also been involved with the man first; because what they had was real love, and she was going to end up marrying him.

"But then he picked me up one day," she said, eyes closed, drifting back in time with the memories, "and took me to Miguel Ángel Sanchez. I told him no, I didn't want to go, but he got real mad, told me to shut up and do what he said." She still looked hurt as she remembered that night, the night she had gone missing, and I couldn't blame her. Betrayal was a hard thing to get over.

"I'd always thought Santiago was strong, you know, a real man. But he was *terrified* by Sanchez, and gave me up in the blink of an eye." She shook her head sadly. "Santiago left, couldn't wait to get out of there, and Sanchez drove me up to this place out in the countryside. A horrible place." She shook her head again, perhaps still unable to believe it. "It was like a warehouse, right? And inside, there were people being *tortured*. And I mean really tortured, not just beaten up. Members of a small local gang who weren't kicking back to the cartel. Sanchez wanted information, you know – who were they working for, was it the Sinaloa, the Gulf, the Tijuana cartel? Which one? Which one?

"And everywhere I looked, there was blood everywhere, they were using everything they had on these guys, there were fingers on the floor that had been hacked off, one guy with a screwdriver right through his eye, they were using a blowtorch on this other man, burning his dick, his balls – and the sound of *screaming*, damn, I thought I'd never be able to hear anything again.

"Sanchez kept me there, made me watch as he tortured some of the guys himself. But in the end, there was nothing to it, they were just a local crew who hadn't wanted to pay Los Zetas their cut. There was no other cartel behind them, none at all.

"But the gang had still crossed the Z's, and the men couldn't live after that, you know? So all that was left was for them to be executed. Hell, most of them were half-dead by then anyway, and some of them were *begging* to be killed.

"Anyway, Sanchez, you know, he puts this big old pearl-handled pistol in my hand, and tells me to shoot them. I look at him as if he's crazy, but he says I have a choice – I can either kill the guys he's been torturing, or else I can join them, and he'll let his men fuck me first, *before* they torture me. I can see the looks on his men's faces, they want to do it, you know? They're *waiting* to do it."

She shook her head, a tear running down her cheek, across the tattooed tears that permanently marked her face.

She looked up at me then, as if daring me to defy her. "So what could I do? I just grabbed that gun and started shooting. One, two, three, four, five! Five men, and I shot them, I fucking shot them, just thirteen fuckin' years old, what the fuck?"

The tears came in force now, her body wracked with sobs, and I moved toward her instinctively; the real Elena Rosales was here now, I was sure of that.

I took a knife and cut the duct tape that held her wrists and ankles, loosened the ropes that held her to the chair, and wrapped my arms around her, protecting her, letting the evils of her past ride out of her body, her mind, her soul.

"I was taken for training after that," she managed between sobs, "like military training. How to kill, how to escape." I felt her tears on my shoulders, and held her closer. "I started again soon enough, started killing. Who'd suspect a teenage girl, huh? That was why Sanchez wanted me, someone the police there didn't know, someone who could easily come and go across the border. He got me hooked on speed, then coke, and I killed for him again and again, kept killing to get my fix."

She broke down again, her body shuddering with the force of her tears, letting it all out, the horror that had been her life.

"I don't even know how many there have been," she wept, hands gripping my arms, head in my chest. "I can't even count the number of people I've killed. There's no hope for me . . . no forgiveness . . . no mercy."

"Elena," I said, "don't say that. You're still young, you can get over this, you'll see. It doesn't have to be like that. Your parents will help you, support you. It's over. It's over."

She giggled then, and the change in demeanor startled me. "You dumb motherfucker," she whispered. "It's never over."

The pain was as intense as it was instantaneous, her fingers snaking up my shoulders, nails ripping into my ears as she held my head steady, her face whipping up, mouth open, teeth sinking deep into my cheek, head thrashing from left to right like a dog with a bone.

I wanted to scream, but couldn't even do that, the pain and shock were so intense, and all I could do was gasp as her nails raked their way across my neck, my face, my eyes.

I was starting to black out from the pain, lids firmly closed to protect my eyeballs from her sharp nails, and I saw stars behind them and felt myself slipping away.

But my instinct for self-preservation was more powerful still, and I refused to give into the pain and – even as she let go of my cheek and latched instead onto my nose, the pain savage and nauseating as her teeth sank deep into the cartilage – I lifted her featherweight body off the floor and ran her backwards, smashing her into the wall.

I felt the breath escape her, but she was still biting, nose clenched tight between sharp teeth; I felt her nails drop from my face, and I opened my eyes, to be met with the horrifying sight of those lifeless tattooed eyeballs on her closed lids.

Inhuman.

Demonic.

I felt myself slipping into unconsciousness, felt the skin of my nose breaking and tearing, the entire thing threatening to come off; and then with one last, frantic effort, I drew my head back, her teeth still attached to my nose, and then drove it forward as hard as I could, smashing the back of *her* head straight into the wall behind her.

Pain raced through my face as her teeth clenched even tighter at the moment of impact; but then her mouth opened and her teeth let go, blood dribbling down onto my chest, covering her face, and her body went slack in my arms.

I looked behind her, saw the bloody smear on the wall where her skull had made impact, and knew she was out for the count, perhaps permanently.

I let her drop to the floor, and – blood still leaking wildly from my damaged face – I checked her pulse. It was weak, but still there; she was still alive.

At least, the cold-blooded sicario known as Z13 was still alive.

But Elena Maria Rosales was dead and gone.

EPILOGUE

"I don't believe it," said Emilio Rosales as he looked from his unconscious daughter to my half-ruined face, and back again. Camila just sat on the bed crying, head in her hands.

I'd called them up as soon as I'd administered a bit of first aid to myself, telling them to get down here. They'd told me that Kane was at their apartment, and I'd told them to bring him along too. I could use a friend, I told myself; it had been a hell of a day.

Emilio hadn't even recognized the girl who had once been his daughter, at first point-blank refusing to believe it was her. Where had his little Elena gone, the apple of daddy's eye?

But Camila had known, and had immediately started to break down and cry – and that was before I'd told them my story.

After they'd been told about the fate of Elena, their distress had been too great to imagine, the polarity of the day's experiences too much to reconcile. Here she was, the girl they'd been searching for, hoping for, praying for, every hour of every day for the past three years and more. Here she was, safe and sound, returned to them at last.

But what was she, really? A killer, a monster – and a seemingly unrepentant one at that. It might have been better if I'd found her dead body, in a grave out in the Mexican countryside.

It would have perhaps been less painful than what they were faced with here.

My story told, my job done, I left them alone there in that room, alone with their daughter as they waited for her to wake up.

I left the room, left the hostel, Kane at my side, licking my hands. I stopped in the street outside, bent at the knees to rub him under the chin. With a look of what seemed to be concern he leaned into me and licked the wounds on my face, but it was too painful and I pulled back, stood up.

"A little early for that," I told him. "But I appreciate the gesture."

I walked across the street with him, bought a cup of coffee from a street vendor and sat down in one of the collapsible metal chairs stationed next to his little stall.

I was curious.

Would Emilio and Camila do the right thing?

It all depended, of course, on what they thought the right thing was. It can be confusing for parents sometimes. Emotions get in the way.

I stayed to watch, to see what would happen, just in case a more logical train of thought was needed.

Just because I'd carried out the job successfully didn't mean that my interest in the case was over – I sure as hell didn't want a killer like Z13 walking free about the streets.

The only question would be who made the call first.

I was on my third coffee by the time I heard the sirens, and had finished it by the time the squad cars arrived outside the hostel.

I saw the cops enter the building, guns drawn, and felt myself relax.

Minutes later, the cops returned, the violently resisting body of Z13 between them, wrestled into one of the waiting cars as her parents looked on, Camila's head on her husband's chest, both of them weeping uncontrollably, unable to process what had happened, what they had learned that day.

I nodded in satisfaction, paid my bill, and stood.

Elena's parents had done the right thing.

Good for them.

I whistled, and Kane popped up by my side, ready to follow.

We meandered through the streets for a time, and I considered getting medical attention for the bites. But I didn't want to come across any radar screens, and just bought some supplies to take care of the wounds myself.

I patched myself up in the train station men's room, then retrieved my backpack from the locker.

I stepped out onto the streets of Laredo, the sun still high in the sky, and sighed.

It had been a hell of a few days, that was for sure.

And I still wasn't sure if they had been successful or not.

But ours is not to reason why, I decided as I set off down the road, Kane by my side.

"Come on boy," I said. "It's only fifty miles or so to the next town."

If we got a move on, we could even by in Corpus Christie within a week, resting up on the beaches of the Gulf of Mexico.

Successful or not, we'd definitely earned it this time.

THE END

. . . but Colt Ryder will return in
THE THOUSAND DOLLAR HUNT

ABOUT THE AUTHOR

J.T. Brannan is the author of the Amazon bestselling political thriller series featuring Mark Cole, as well as the high-concept thrillers ORIGIN (translated into eight languages in over thirty territories) and EXTINCTION (his latest all-action novel from Headline Publishing), in addition to the sci-fi action short story DESTRUCTIVE THOUGHTS.

THE THOUSAND DOLLAR MAN – the first novel to feature his new hero, Colt Ryder - was nominated for the 2016 Killer Nashville Silver Falchion Award.

Currently serving in the British Army Reserves, J.T. Brannan is a former national Karate champion and bouncer.

He now writes full-time, and teaches martial arts in Harrogate, in the North of England, where he lives with his wife and two young children.

He is currently working on the next novel in the bestselling Mark Cole series, as well as further books in the all-new Colt Ryder series.

You can find him at www.jtbrannan.com and www.jtbrannanbooks.blogspot.com, on Twitter @JTBrannan_, and on Facebook at jtbrannanbooks

ALSO BY THE AUTHOR

The Colt Ryder series:
THE THOUSAND DOLLAR MAN
THE THOUSAND DOLLAR HUNT
THE THOUSAND DOLLAR ESCAPE
THE THOUSAND DOLLAR CONTRACT
Colt Ryder Short Story:
THE THOUSAND DOLLAR CHRISTMAS

The Mark Cole series:
STOP AT NOTHING
WHATEVER THE COST
BEYOND ALL LIMITS
NEVER SAY DIE
PLEDGE OF HONOR
THE LONE PATRIOT

Alternative Mark Cole thriller:
SEVEN DAY HERO

Other Novels:
ORIGIN
EXTINCTION
TIME QUEST

Short Story:
DESTRUCTIVE THOUGHTS

Made in the USA
Las Vegas, NV
08 February 2022